Nicholas and I looked at each other, then back at the tall guy. There was something about him, something familiar. . . .

Then all of a sudden it hit me. My stomach felt like a Slinky that had just spilled to the ground and sprung up again. My knees felt like Slinkies too, all stretchy-wobbly, but I grabbed Vivian and started walking as fast as I could down a side street, away from the tall guy and the Video Barn.

Nicholas ran up behind us. "What's going on?"

I know who he is, I mouthed over Vivian's head so she wouldn't hear me.

Who? Nicholas mouthed back.

I looked down at Vivi walking between us, jumping over cracks in the sidewalk, then at Nicholas.

My father.

ALSO AVAILABLE FROM DELL LAUREL-LEAF BOOKS

beth cooley

ostrich
eye

Published by
Dell Laurel-Leaf
an imprint of
Random House Children's Books
a division of Random House, Inc.
New York

Visit us on the Web! www.randomhouse.com/teens

Educators and librarians, for a variety of teaching tools, visit us at www.randomhouse.com/teachers

ISBN: 0-440-23828-5

RL: 4.8

Reprinted by arrangement with Delacorte Press

Printed in the United States of America

First Dell Laurel-Leaf Edition July 2005

10 9 8 7 6 5 4 3 2 1

OPM

Thanks to Sarah Conover, Laura Read, Nadine Chapman, Patricia Terry, and Betty Wayne Cooley for their support; to Stella Kent, Jim Lipp, Josie Cooley, and Jess Walter for their expertise; to Kathy Williamson for planting the seed for this novel and to Mary Cronk Farrell for telling me what to do with it once it was finished; to Wendy Loggia for her insight and invaluable suggestions; and finally to my family—Dan, Bess, and Emma.

for bess and emma

chapter 1

every time I try to figure out how it all started, I find myself going back to that really nice stretch of days last spring. It was one of those early May afternoons when the birds are kind of flowing in waves from one backyard to the next, eating all the birdseed at one feeder, then moving on. When the lilacs are starting to bud and the lettuce in the gardens is coming up in pale green stripes and you tie your sweater around your waist and let your arms soak up some sun.

I'd gotten off the school bus in front of Kim's house as usual and walked the two blocks home. As I went in the front door, I heard Mom talking in the kitchen.

"God knows how much I hate crafts," she was saying. "A glue gun makes me want to break out in hives." At first I thought she was talking to me, but then I heard my aunt Suzanne's quick bright voice and smelled the coffee and cinnamon rolls.

"Couldn't you get somebody else to do it?" Suzanne asked.

"I've called everybody. Everybody's too busy."

"Like you're not?" Suzanne said. "You just started a new job, Renee, isn't that enough?" My mom had recently gotten her Realtor's license and was out at all hours of the day and night showing houses.

"True," Mom said. "But Vivian really wants to be a Sunbeam Scout. How much trouble could becoming a troop leader be, anyhow?"

It was a good question. My mom is the last person you'd expect to volunteer. She hates camping, is useless at crafts, and is about as organized as a pile of leaves. She's hardly ever on time and loses things like her car keys or even the car itself if I don't remind her where she parked when we come out of the mall. I doubt she knows the Pledge of Allegiance, and because of her Catholic-school upbringing, she is totally against uniforms. She went on and on about them when I said I might want to join marching band. Like you can have a halftime show without uniforms. On the other hand, that she would become a troop leader just because my half sister, Vivian, wanted to be a Sunbeam Scout was no surprise at all. She'll do anything for Vivian.

"Once a week, Kool-Aid and cookies," Mom went on. "Ginger can help me with the crafts. She likes that kind of thing."

2

"Ginger is just as busy as anybody else," I mumbled to myself, and dropped my backpack, loud, on the tile floor of our entryway.

"Gin, is that you?" Mom called from the kitchen. "How was your day? Got any homework?"

"A little," I said as I came into the kitchen and took a cinnamon roll, still warm and gooey, from the box on the table. Suzanne had brought them. Mom doesn't buy stuff like that. To her a snack means an apple or yogurt or at best a granola bar, although I've never seen her pass up a cinnamon roll when it was put in front of her.

"Well, take a little break, get yourself something to eat, and get started with it," she said cheerfully. This conversation was routine. It didn't matter whether I had no homework or about a million pages to read in social studies and a report in English and a boatload of math, which is what I had that afternoon. She always told me to get started with it. And if homework wasn't enough to deal with, in three weeks Cottonwood High School would have its Freshman Spring Fling, which I had absolutely no interest in going to but somehow *was,* thanks to Kim and Annie.

"Hey there, Stringbean," Suzanne said, smiling all crinkle-eyed like she does and calling me by the nickname she gave me when I started kindergarten. I was extremely skinny back then and a good three inches taller than every other kid in the class. "Get yourself a glass of milk to go with that roll. Put some meat on those bones." She still had on her navy blue uniform. Her web gear—a big nylon belt with all the key keepers and gadgets on it—was curled up in the empty chair, and her radio mike was clipped to her shoulder. Suzanne works as a security officer at St. Sebastian College and takes a couple of classes in criminal justice every semester. She wants to be a police detective, even though she's starting kind of late. She's five years younger than Mom, so she'll be thirty next January. Like my mom, she was a little slow in figuring out what she wanted to be when she grew up. Unlike my mom, she'd be the first to admit it.

"Well, I guess that's all settled," Mom said to Suzanne, then turned to me like I'd been part of the discussion all along. "The Rosa girls are ready for scouting."

Suzanne laughed. "But is scouting ready for you?"

•   •   •

As soon as my stepdad, Tony, got home from work that afternoon, Vivian charged him, shouting, "I'm gonna be a Sunbeam! I get to sell cookies!" over and over like a crazy person. Tony picked her up and swung her around. "That's great, big girl. When do you get your beanie?"

"Brownies wear beanies. We get baseball caps."

Tony put his yellow hard hat on her head and swung her around again. Then they both plopped down beside me on the couch, where I was trying to read about China and the Cultural Revolution.

"What's up?" Tony socked me lightly on the arm and put up his fists, dodging like a boxer. "Gotten any taller today? Have you outgrown the man of the house yet?"

"Outgrew him ages ago," I said. It's a running joke between us, but it's also true. Tony's really good-looking, but on the short side. Short, dark, and handsome, as Suzanne

4

says. I'm pushing six feet. I got my height from my real dad, who I don't remember at all. He left for good when I was about three. Tony married Mom when I was in kindergarten. At first he wanted me to call him Dad, but I couldn't do it. Tony has always been just Tony to me. Still, he's the only father I've ever known, and I sure could do a lot worse. He's been at every single school play or basketball game or band concert I've ever participated in. Maybe he used to swing me around like he does Vivi and let me wear his hard hat. I don't remember. We joke around a lot, but I don't think he feels like I'm his real daughter. Nothing against Tony—I know he loves me and all—but when I see how he is with Vivian, there's no comparison.

I was in third grade when Vivian was born. From her first breath, Vivian has been the kind of kid people can't help staring at. I remember looking at her through the glass at the hospital nursery, remember total strangers pointing at her while Tony stood there with a tremendous grin on his face. It still happens. In the grocery store, for instance, people will stand there holding a box of Kix or saltines and just watch her go by like they've forgotten what they're supposed to be doing. The reason is because she's absolutely beautiful. Really. She's petite and dark like Tony but with big deep blue eyes that she got from who knows where—Mom's are gray like mine—and pretty black curls. She takes gymnastics and has perfect little cheerleader legs, with strong calves and tiny ankles. Plus, she's really intelligent, already reading way above second-grade level.

Me, I'm average. I usually get Bs, I'm fifth-chair clarinet in band, and I'm fairly competitive at sports, like basketball. Mainly because I'm half a foot taller than nearly everyone else on the court. I rebound pretty well and usually score once or twice in a game, but I'm a crummy free-throw shooter. I don't draw amazing pictures or make one-of-a-kind outfits like my longtime best friend, Annie, and I'm not a genius like my neighbor and other best friend, Kim, who's in honors classes and goes to this camp for the academically gifted in the summer.

And I don't look or act a thing like Vivian, who had crawled up onto Tony's lap like a cuddly little kitten. Except she was talking, talking, talking. Vivi started talking at eleven months and basically hasn't stopped since. Sometimes it's hard to pay attention to her. She just kind of becomes background noise for everything else that's going on in our house.

"We start Sunbeam meetings next week," Vivi said. "Me and Michaela and Alex and Sarah and Nina and Jaime and Brittany. And Ginger."

"Ginger?"

"Mommy's the big leader and Ginger's the little leader." Vivian hopped off Tony's lap and twirled around the room. "And we get to all dress alike and we can be in the Christmas parade. Alex says that's what you do when you're a Sunbeam Scout."

"Are you sure you have time for this?" Tony asked Mom, who was putting dinner on the table. We were having eggs and toast for the second time that week because she hadn't had a chance to get to the grocery store.

"How much trouble could it be?" she asked, and fluffed her short brown hair with her fingers. This is something my mother does when she feels an argument coming on. It kind of reminds me of the way a chicken puffs up when it feels threatened, though I'd never tell her that. As she fluffed, she launched into the same line she gave Suzanne about once a week and Kool-Aid and me helping out.

"Is this all right with you, Ginger?" Tony asked.

"Of course it's all right with Ginger," Mom said, but Tony waited for me to answer.

"It's okay," I said. He wasn't convinced.

"What if you get paid to help?" he asked, and I perked up a little. "How about five dollars for every meeting and extra for field trips?"

"This is volunteer work," Mom said.

"But Ginger didn't volunteer, did she? She got drafted." He took out his wallet and handed me a five. "Here's an advance. With these latest bids and my wife gainfully employed, I can afford to spread the wealth." This was only partly true. Tony's a contractor, and he's had a lot of work lately, but even with Mom working now, he really can't afford to spread things too far. Nobody ever knows what the housing market will do, he's always saying.

"Don't spend it all in one place," he said, and winked. "Now that I've heard all of Vivian's news, how was your day?"

The real answer to that question was it sucked. But I couldn't tell Tony that, especially not after the money. Being generous made him way too cheerful. Why spoil his mood? So I said what I almost always say, that it was okay, and ate my toast and eggs. After loading the dishwasher, I went down to my bedroom, which is in the basement of our beige sixties ranch house. Tony had put some Latin jazz on the CD player and was cha-chaing Mom around the kitchen. The speakers are situated right over my bed, so I pulled the pink earmuffs I keep on my bedpost (just for these occasions) over my ears and tried to put a dent in my homework. The reasons it sucked— my day, that is—were multiple, but the main reason was because I got asked to the Freshman Spring Fling by Nicholas Blackstone, the weirdest guy at Cottonwood High School.

•   •   •

"Okay, so he's a little different," Annie had said at lunch that day. "But he's cute. I mean look at that wavy black hair, and that skin. I'd kill for his complexion." She ran a finger over some red bumps on her forehead. "See these zits? They spell ACNE in Braille."

"And he's really tall," added Kim, who has an eye for symmetry and proportion.

"And he and Carter are best friends," I said. "Which is the real reason he asked me. Admit it, Kimmy." Carter is Kim's boyfriend, and Kim couldn't go to the dance unless she went with a group. Her parents are super strict. Apparently Nicholas and I, along with Annie and her date, Ryan, would constitute a large enough crowd to suit them.

"Not true," Kim said. "He asked you because he thinks you're hot."

"Look, I said I'd go. You don't have to make things up."

Kim raised an eyebrow. "Who's making things up? Why wouldn't he think you're hot?"

I didn't bother to answer. The only thing approaching

hot about me is my name, which, as people love to remind me, is also the name of the airhead movie star on that old TV show *Gilligan's Island*. You can see the reruns on cable. Mom says she named me in hopes that I'd keep the ginger red hair I was born with. Unfortunately, it faded to dead-leaf brown at six months and has stayed that way ever since.

"You never give yourself enough credit," Kim said, pushing her own copper curls off her forehead. She would have gone on about my so-called inferiority complex, one of her favorite subjects, if Annie hadn't asked what I was going to wear.

"I haven't thought about it," I mumbled. Annie had been working for weeks on her dress, an incredible beaded black satin number that I couldn't believe she made herself.

"The dance is in three weeks and you haven't thought about it?" She was appalled.

"Look," I said, "I didn't even have a date until second period. And even then I wasn't sure what Nicholas was trying to say." He had started out by quoting a poem or asking a riddle; I couldn't tell which. When I didn't get it, he turned bright red and asked me to the dance like a normal person. I was so shocked I said yes.

"Don't worry about what to wear," Annie said. "We'll help you find something stunning."

"And don't worry about Nicholas," Kim added. "He's just a little unique."

"A little unique? What about the time in fifth grade when he put that cricket in his mouth just to prove insects weren't as dirty as everybody thought?"

"I'd call that unique," Annie said, making a face. "Totally disgusting, but unique."

"And what about seventh grade when he wore that kilt to school day after day, even after Miles Conrad and those guys wrote *fag* on his locker?" I asked.

"Even after Mrs. White told him that if he was going to wear a skirt he'd have to keep his knees together," Annie added. She couldn't help herself.

"That took some courage, don't you think?" Kim said, and gave Annie a sharp look. "It says something about his character."

"Yeah, that he's totally bizarre," I said.

"Besides, that was a long time ago. He's matured since then."

"Two years is all. Two years ago the guy I'm going to the dance with wore a skirt to school."

"Kilt. They're called kilts," Kim said.

"Hey, Mel Gibson rode horses in one," Annie chimed in. "In *Braveheart*? You'd never call him a weirdo."

"That's the movies, you guys," I said. "What we're talking about here is my life."

•   •   •

"So how's scouting?" Annie asked a week later. We were running in Curry Park, something we did religiously. As soon as the snow started melting in early March, Kim had decided we all needed to get in shape. While Annie was running to firm up what she called her thunder thighs and Kim was trying to lose five pounds before the Spring Fling, I ran because I liked it.

"Scouting's okay," I said. "We meet in the basement of the Methodist church. We've only had a couple of meetings, but so far, it's easy enough." During the first meeting the Sunbeams got their yellow caps and blue vests and learned the "Sunbeam Smile Song." A bunch of Moms were there with camcorders, so I pretty much just sat and watched. Even though I could think of at least six places I'd rather be, it was an easy five dollars.

"What do you do with all those little kids?" Kim asked.

"Pour Kool-Aid and clean up spills. Last time they practiced songs for this trip they're taking to a retirement center. Suzanne came by and played the piano for us."

Annie giggled. "Sounds fascinating."

"Hey, I get paid." Enough for a third of a CD, I thought, but didn't say it.

"So what are you wearing?"

"To scout meetings?"

"No, silly. To the dance."

"God, Annie, don't you have other things to think about?"

"You know, you're really lucky to be going out with him," Kim said. Again. She'd been telling me several times a day how wonderful Nicholas was. "He's got a great sense of humor."

"How do you know?" I asked.

"Carter says so."

"Carter. Well, no bias there!" I said, and sprinted ahead.

Curry Park is a good place to run, with lots of gardens and play areas. In the center is a big pond where ducks—and for a few weeks in the spring and fall, Canadian geese—paddle around and eat stale bread tossed by little kids and old ladies with small fluffy dogs. Kim had mapped out a two-mile route that took us through the rose garden, past the playground, around the duck pond, and then back by each of our houses. Annie used our run to give her dogs some exercise. Her mom has two huge malamutes, and they kept us going at a pretty good pace.

I was in good shape from basketball season and my legs are long, so I found myself kind of jogging along with the dogs while Kim and Annie were huffing and puffing to keep up with us. I doubled back to let them catch up.

"It's not fair," Kim said, blowing her curls off her forehead. "Ginger has to take only half as many steps as I do, therefore I'm expending twice as much energy."

"That's why I double back," I laughed. No matter what Kim's talking about, she sounds like a textbook. "Just to make this little jog worthwhile."

"Oh, please," Annie gasped. Even her long blond ponytail looked worn out.

It had rained the night before and everything looked washed clean. The rhododendrons were blooming magenta, lavender, and coral, and down by the pond the willows swayed lacy green wands over the dark water. Ducks glided silently, and a blue heron stood motionless beside a log. The sun was warm, the air was cool, and I felt like I could run forever.

We were heading along the far end of the pond when I noticed this guy sitting on top of one of the concrete picnic tables, his feet resting on a bench. He was tall and lanky and wore a fringed brown suede jacket. He had a bandana tied over his long blond hair. Even with his weird seventies-style clothes, I don't think he would have registered except for the way he was staring at us. Not the sneaky kind of staring guys do when they try to pretend they're really looking at something else, but the kind of staring guys do when they're watching a sporting event. Focused. It was almost as if he were taking aim as we jogged along the shore. His intense attitude made me nervous, and I sped up.

"Slow down! This is not a race," Annie called out. "What—are we starting to sprint now, too?"

"Sorry," I said, and moved around her so I could keep an eye on the guy. He never took his eyes off us; his head swiveled slowly like it was on ball bearings until we were out of sight.

•　•　•

"Did you notice that guy in the park?" I asked Kim and Annie after our run. We were sitting on the deck at my house, cooling down with glasses of iced tea and eating a bowl of trail mix, which my mom makes by the five-gallon tub and always has on hand.

"What guy?" Kim said.

"Sitting on the picnic table by the pond."

"Why, was he cute?"

"No, not that. He was older. I mean much older, thirty at least," I said. "He was scoping us out, and he seemed to be awfully interested in what he saw."

"Well, he ought to be!" Annie laughed, tossing her long blond hair. "We're a pretty good-looking bunch."

"Middle-aged men are always attracted to adolescent girls," Kim added. "It's biological. That's why so many of them leave their wives, who are approaching menopause, and go for younger, more fertile women."

"That's gross," Annie said.

I took a sip of my tea. "Yeah, but there was something about him . . . like he really shouldn't have been in Curry Park at all."

Just then Mom came out on the deck with the tea pitcher and her industrial-size container of trail mix. "I'm sure he had every right to be in Curry Park," she said lightly. That's the thing about parents. You think you're carrying on a private conversation with your friends and then they chime in out of nowhere. They don't even hear half the conversation, but they've got to give you their opinion. "He might not fit the profile of the Curry Park neighborhood, but that doesn't mean he can't enjoy the gardens. Last time I checked it was still public property."

"I know, Mom. I'm not saying he shouldn't be allowed there. I'm just saying he didn't look like he fit in. He gave me the creeps staring at us like that."

"How do you know for sure he was staring at you?" Mom retorted. "Maybe he was looking at the ducks. You know, it's not always all about you." She laughed, but her laugh had an edge.

"Forget it," I said. Kim gazed off across the backyard, and Annie looked like she might go into one of her giggling fits. Mom poured more trail mix into our bowl and went back inside.

"I'm not blind," I said after she'd closed the sliding glass door behind her. "That man definitely was not looking at the ducks."

chapter 2

the following Tuesday the Sunbeam Scouts piled into Mom's van and Suzanne's red convertible—which of course they all wanted to ride in—and we drove to Holly Hills Retirement Center. Mom had corralled Suzanne into coming along to play piano. Suzanne can actually play really well. She's got a regular Thursday-night gig at the Sheraton lounge and takes any opportunity she can to perform. But she might have thought twice about playing at Holly Hills if she'd had a chance to check out their piano. It was a battered upright from about the eighteenth century. It was way out of tune, and some of the lower notes wouldn't sound at all, but Suzanne gave the retirees her Sheraton smile and did her best.

Running through a bunch of patriotic songs and ending with "He's Got the Whole World in His Hands," the Sunbeams sang in clear high voices and didn't seem to notice the sour piano. Neither did the folks out there at Holly Hills. In fact, some of them slept right through the whole performance only to wake up and clap at the end. A couple of old ladies would not stop talking the whole time, like the Sunbeams weren't even there, but most of the residents paid attention, and one or two wiped their eyes the way old people do when they see a group of little kids. It must be hard on them to see children with their whole lives ahead of them when any one of them—the old people, I mean—could go to bed at night and not wake up the next morning. It's no wonder some of them check out by falling asleep or pretending no one is there.

After the performance we were treated to Oreos and Sprite, and the old ladies took turns holding hands with the Sunbeams and telling them how sweet they sounded. The Sunbeams tolerated the attention—I think they felt more like well-behaved cats than little girls—and then we left.

"I'm not sure taking the Sunbeams to Holly Hills was such a good thing to do," I said to Mom as we drove home. Seven of the girls were in the back of the van giggling. The other four were right behind us in Suzanne's convertible, waving at everyone who passed.

"What a negative thing to say." Mom glanced at her rearview mirror to make sure the Sunbeams hadn't heard me, but Vivi and her friends were playing telephone and paying no attention to us.

"It just seems kind of cruel to remind those senior citizens of what's behind them," I said.

"Mrs. Torres said they just loved it."

"Mrs. Torres is the director. She has to say things like that."

Mom shook her head and sighed one of her suffering-mother sighs. "I don't know why you have to be so negative. Those folks at Holly Hills loved it, and it was a good experience for the girls. They need to see all kinds of people. It broadens their horizons."

"Red light," I said, and braced my feet against the floor of the van. Maybe I should have waited until we were safely off the streets before bringing up the subject.

"I see the red light," Mom said as we jerked to a stop. "That's one thing that's wrong with our society," she went on.

"Red lights?"

"No. Segregation. We're all separated from each other. Age, class, race, religion. How many old people, truly old people, do you know?"

I shrugged. "Gramma Pearce? Tony's dad?"

"They're in their early sixties. That is not old. And besides, you don't really know them. You see them about twice a year when they come to visit."

"Okay, you're right. I don't know any old people." That wasn't the point I was trying to make, but she had that tone of voice like she was talking with earphones on and couldn't really hear what I was saying. It was better just to let her finish her lecture. The real point for me was that people don't like to be reminded about what they haven't got. A clunky piano, an ugly building, and too many TVs, that's what the people at Holly Hills have. Those high little voices singing about God having little bitty babies in his hands is what they don't have. And it seemed to me they didn't need to be reminded of that. But apparently Mom didn't care to consider that point. She was too busy helping the Sunbeams rack up their citizenship badges.

After Holly Hills I hoped that somebody with a glue gun would show up so Sunbeam Scout Troop 456 could get on with normal Sunbeam activities, like Mexican yarn painting or making sit-upons, but I had no such luck. Mom had latched on to the two-pronged idea that the Sunbeams needed to broaden their horizons and save the world. And she wouldn't let go.

●　　●　　●

During the three weeks before the Spring Fling, Nicholas Blackstone spoke to me maybe two times. That doesn't count mumbling hi and grinning and turning red when he passed me in the hall, which made me mumble hi and grin and turn red too. I had to admit, to myself if not to Kim, that he was kind of cute when he blushed. His cheeks turned a nice shade of pink and his eyes got all sparkly under his floppy bangs. Still. One of those two times when he said more than hi was at lunch when he presented me with a mango and said something in Spanish. At least I think it was Spanish. The second time he stopped by my locker to tell me about slugbots, robots powered by slug meat, and flatulence engines, robots powered by gas produced from the vegetable matter they ingested. They'd be perfect for lawn care, he said, if scientists could just get the bugs out. Get it?

Anyway, Nicholas was so goofy that I didn't really get nervous about the dance. *He* might be socially challenged, but *I* could still have a good time with my friends. I was all ready for it: new dress (blue), nail polish and lip gloss to match (pale pink—the only color Mom finally approved of), cool shoes (Suzanne's), and one of those carnation boutonniere things to go on Nicholas's lapel. Because of some ancient Spring Fling tradition, the boys were all required to wear dress pants and jackets.

At least that ruled out a kilt.

•   •   •

School let out at noon on Friday, the day of the dance. Technically this was for a teachers' planning session, but everybody knew it was really to let the decoration committee finish up in the gym and to give the faculty a rest before they had to come back and chaperone. I carted all my stuff over to Annie's right after school. Annie's sister, Amber, who's going to cosmetology school, was doing this kind of personal spa with us—facials, hair, manicures, pedicures, and makeup. Amber is really good at what she does. Everybody in Annie's family has great haircuts. So what happened wasn't really her fault. In fact, most of the spa treatment was wonderful. She gave me a lavender-mint aromatherapy scalp massage and shampooed and conditioned my hair. She did my nails and got the scaly skin off my heels with pumice stone, which was kind of unnecessary since I wasn't wearing sandals but which felt good anyway.

Once our hands and feet were all done and our hair was

wrapped in fluffy cotton towels, Amber announced it was time for our mud therapy. She made us lie down on warm towels on the floor and opened a big jar of gooey blue stuff.

"I'll just smooth this on your face and you can relax and listen to the sounds of nature." She turned on her CD player, and we could hear something moaning over a background of violins. Kim giggled.

"Whales," Annie said, rolling her eyes as Amber began globbing what looked like turquoise mayonnaise on her face. Amber has this thing for sea mammals—dolphins, whales, manatees. If it has hair and swims, she loves it.

"This stays on for fifteen minutes," she said after we were iced up like blueberry cakes.

"What's in it?" Kim asked, wrinkling her nose. "Smells like the mudpots at Yellowstone."

"Don't do that!" Amber smoothed the goop over Kim's nose again. "You have to let it harden without moving a muscle."

Of course, that was all it took. Kim's shoulders started shaking and Annie snorted, and I couldn't keep from laughing either.

"This treatment is really expensive at the salon, you guys, so don't blow it." Amber stood there with her hands on her hips. A noise remarkably like a whale call escaped from Kim.

"I mean it," Amber said, setting a kitchen timer for fifteen minutes. "I'm not doing anybody over again. When I get back, I expect no cracks."

Once she left the room, we settled down. The whale music was weird but soothing, and I nearly fell asleep feeling the blue goop tingling into my skin. I was actually starting to look forward to the evening. My dress was a cornflower shade that made my gray eyes look almost blue. Amber was going to French-braid my hair and tuck little silk flowers around the edges. Lying there nearly asleep, listening to whales, I could even imagine dancing, not with Nicholas, but with some handsome stranger, tall, blond, broad shouldered. My dress flowed around my knees; my feet were light and quick, my hair lustrous. When the buzzer went off, I nearly jumped out of my skin.

"Okay, time to rinse off," Amber said. I tried to open my eyes but couldn't. Okay, I'm still asleep, I thought, and tried to open them again like you do when you know you're dreaming and can't get your eyelids to work. And then I realized my eyes *were* open—at least, as open as they could get.

"Oh my god," Amber said, grabbing my arm and pulling me up off the floor. "Turn on the shower, Annie. We've got some kind of allergic reaction here."

Until the blue goop I had never been allergic to anything in my life, but was I ever allergic this time. My face was like a pink balloon. It didn't hurt, it didn't itch, it just swelled and swelled and swelled until they got me to the emergency room and the doctor hooked me up to an IV with Benadryl or something in it. Tony came to the hospital as soon as Annie called—Mom was out showing a house—and he sat with me until the swelling started to go down and he could take me home. When we went in the front door, Vivian was momentarily speechless, but Mom, who had canceled her appointments and rushed home, had plenty to say.

"I told you about using makeup."

"It wasn't makeup, it was mud therapy."

"Until Amber is a licensed therapist, no more skin treatments." Mom shook her head. "You don't need them, anyhow, at your age. You have beautiful skin. Or had."

"Renee," Tony said. "She had no idea this would happen. The doctor said she should be fine in twenty-four hours, maybe even by tomorrow morning. Believe me, she already looks much better."

"She does?" Vivian finally found her tongue. "How fat was her face before?"

"Just shut up!" I shouted.

"Ginger, do not shout at your sister!" Mom said. Shouted, actually. Vivian stuck out her tongue.

"It's not like I did this on purpose!" I cried. "You think I did this just for fun?" I ran down the stairs to my bedroom and slammed the door. The face in my dresser mirror was the ugliest face I'd ever seen. Red and puffy with dull gray eyes sunk deep into burned-looking skin, all framed by limp, tangled hair. And I had actually thought I could look pretty that night. Or at least above average.

When the phone rang, I didn't bother to answer it. I knew it would be Kim and Annie calling from the dance to see how I was doing. Tony or Mom could talk to them. Tony or Mom could tell Nicholas his date looked like a giant blister ready to pop. It kind of surprised me how disappointed I was. I hadn't realized how much I really wanted to be there, how much I actually wanted to be with Nicholas.

Maybe it was the allergy medicine, but I hardly moved a muscle for what seemed like hours, just lay on my bed watching nothing out of my small, high bedroom win-

dows. Having a room in the basement gives me a lot of privacy, but sometimes it gets kind of lonely. Right now I was
thankful for the privacy, but a little lonesome too, so I was
glad when Tony knocked on my door with a small veggie
pizza and a bottle of guava juice.

"Special delivery." He put the pizza, still steaming hot,
on my desk. "You're looking a lot better."

"But I'm missing the dance."

"The whole gang was on the phone a little while ago
asking about you. I didn't think you wanted to talk."

"Thanks."

"That Nicholas seems like a nice fellow. He said he'd
call you tomorrow, if that's okay."

"Sure, whatever."

"Need anything else?" I shook my head. "Your mom
will be down to say good night in a little while. She's getting Vivian to bed."

"That's okay. She doesn't have to."

"She wants to, Ginger." He blew a puff of air between
his lips and shook his head. "You two."

"Us two what?" I said.

"You and your mother, you're so much alike."

Great, I thought. The perfect ending to a perfect day.

●　　●　　●

Of course, Mom had to come down after that. She
brought me another bottle of juice, cranberry this time,
and a new *Seventeen* magazine. I accepted the magazine for
the peace offering it was. As a rule, she disapproves of
what she calls popular-culture garbage.

"Feeling okay?" she asked, putting her hand on my forehead like she used to when I was little.

"Yeah."

"Can I get you anything else?"

"I'm okay."

She put both hands on my cheeks for a minute. Her fingers were smooth and cool. Then her forehead creased in a worried frown. "Well, I guess this was a lesson learned."

I didn't say anything. Leave it to Mom to turn a sympathy visit into a teachable moment.

"And you'll be sure to get Suzanne's shoes back from Annie's ASAP, won't you?"

I nodded and pulled my earmuffs off the bedpost as she left the room.

•   •   •

It was after eleven when I woke up the next morning. I ran my fingers over my face. It felt smooth, except for the usual zits, so I looked in the mirror, and sure enough, everything was back to normal. Longish nose, gray eyes, thick eyebrows, a completely average mouth, a chin dimple. Not a great face, but a huge improvement over the one I saw in the same mirror last night.

"Hey, Ginger, you don't look fat anymore." Vivian greeted me in her loud chipper voice when I came into the kitchen. She was filling a large bowl with Froot Loops. "Mommy and Daddy went to shop for a snow blower. You're supposed to baby-sit me."

Only my parents would go snowblower shopping in

May. Must be a clearance sale. "Be careful with that," I warned Vivi just as she overshot her cereal bowl and sloshed milk onto the counter. "Jeez, Viv, couldn't you just ask?"

"A Sunbeam Scout is self-reliant. That means I can do it myself."

"Yeah? Well, apparently not. Here, let me wipe it up before it drips on the floor."

"Oh yeah. I was supposed to tell you somebody came by to see you."

"Who?" I said, sopping up milk.

"I forget."

"Kim? Annie?"

"It was a boy. He looked like this." She pulled her lips into a thin, straight line and flared her nostrils slightly in an amazing imitation of Nicholas. "He said he'd see you later."

"Later when? Today later?"

"I don't know. Sometime." She began pirouetting across the kitchen floor, then stopped suddenly and pointed out the window. "Look, that's him now."

"Oh my god, Vivi, get away from that window." But it was too late. She was waving like a maniac. Nicholas coasted up the driveway on his bike, threw his long leg over the seat, and came to a graceful stop right in front of the door, which Vivi had already opened.

"Hey there!" she shouted. "Ginger finally dragged herself out of bed!"

"Hey there yourself." Nicholas pushed his wild black curls out of his eyes and grinned at Vivi. He held a small white box in his right hand. "Where's your sister?"

I stepped into the doorway, wishing I had on something

besides a Winnie-the-Pooh T-shirt and plaid flannel boxers. Quickly, I pulled off my pink earmuffs and dropped them on the floor behind me, hoping that somehow miraculously Nicholas hadn't noticed.

"This is for you." He bowed and handed me the white box. "I was supposed to give it to you last night, but, well, better late than never." Inside was a corsage of pink sweetheart roses. It would have looked great with the blue dress I'd probably never have a chance to wear. I thanked him, and we stood on the porch looking down at each other's feet until I managed to come up with something intelligent to say.

"So, how was the dance, anyway?"

"Okay, I guess. I didn't stay real long."

What was I supposed to say to that? Was he glad he didn't have to stay long? Was he ticked off because his date had a medical emergency? Did he find someone else to dance with? Does he even like to dance?

"The DJ was pretty cool," he said. "Lots of variety."

"That's good."

He said something about the decorations and I said something back, and then he said, "Well, I guess I better go."

Despite my appearance, I didn't want him to go, but I couldn't very well keep him standing there for no good reason.

"Thanks again for the flowers. Sorry about the dance."

"Hey, don't worry about that. I'm just glad you're feeling better." He smiled again and really looked at me. I really looked at him too, maybe for the first time ever. His eyes were green, flecked with gold like sunlight on water. Fabulous! How could I have missed noticing them before?

"Maybe we could do something else sometime," he said, and flung his leg over his bicycle. "I'll call you?"

"Sure. Okay. That would be great." I hoped he knew I meant it. I stood on the porch until he sailed around the corner, and held the corsage close to my face. It smelled cool and sweet like a florist shop, the buds a perfect pink. Our whole conversation had lasted less than five minutes, but it had made me consider Nicholas Blackstone in a totally new light.

chapter 3

for their last meeting in May the Sunbeams were taking May baskets to the pediatric ward at St. Clair's Hospital. St. Clair's handles everything from broken bones to genetic disorders to terminal illnesses. Kids from all over the Northwest seek specialized treatment there, and Mom thought it would be nice for the Sunbeams to contribute in some way.

Anyhow, the night before their visit, Mom and I sat at the kitchen table gluing ribbons onto Chinese take-out boxes. Mr. Wong had donated the boxes last time we picked up dinner at the Wok-n-Roll. People were always giving Mom things for the Sunbeams—ends of butcher paper, leftover mat board, old wallpaper sample books. Of course, since the Sunbeams spent all their time being good citizens instead of making crafts, the stuff was accumulating. Mostly in the basement. Mom's a natural pack rat, and she just can't turn down an offer. At least the take-out boxes would be put to good use. Or some kind of use.

"You know, May's almost over," I reminded Mom, who was counting four-packs of blue and yellow pansies.

She nodded. "Only six days left."

"Well, you give May baskets on May Day, right? That's May first, not May twenty-fifth."

"You're missing the point, Ginger," Mom said. Seems like that's about all we did with each other lately, miss the point. She missed my point; I missed her point. We were like two arrows that were supposed to match up in a diagram, but the instructions were all wrong.

"Besides," I went on, though I knew it was futile, "I'm not so sure this good deed for St. Clair's is such a good idea." I cut a piece of yellow ribbon and glued it to a take-out box. "I mean, taking a bunch of healthy children to visit a bunch of seriously unhealthy children . . ."

"Have I heard this argument before?" Mom asked. "Let's see. I heard it at Holly Hills, am I right? People only get more unhappy when they see what they don't have, right? Well, I happen to disagree."

"How could it make sick kids feel better to see Vivian and her friends running around so happy and energetic when they've got all kinds of problems?"

"Maybe it will give them hope that someday they'll be running around too."

"But they won't be. That's the point. A lot of those kids at St. Clair's will never be normal."

"How do you define normal?" Mom asked, ruffling her fingers through her short hair. "Perfect?" She was on the verge of puffing up like a mad hen. "The point is, they need to know somebody cares about them."

This was going nowhere fast, so I kept quiet. In a minute she held up her take-out May basket. The bow sat at a funny angle, and glue dripped down the side. "Your baskets look so much neater than mine. Your bows are so perky."

I sighed. "Just leave the rest for me." It wasn't that big a chore, really; it was the principle of the thing that got me. Mom had taken on this Sunbeam project, and here I was doing most of the work. I was beginning to understand something about my mother. She had good intentions; she really cared about helping people and making the world a better place—theoretically. But when it came to the nuts and bolts of getting stuff done, she was pretty incompetent. At least, that was what it felt like to me.

When the phone rang five minutes later, Mom jumped up to get it. "Hi, Joyce," she said, smiling. "Yes, that's the plan. We'll leave from the Methodist church, visit St. Clair's, and have them all home by dinnertime." She paused, and I knew something was up. "I'm sorry to hear that. Well, we'll miss Brittany, and Michaela too. You tell Marie I said so, okay?"

She hung up. "I thought I'd run into this, but not from Joyce Davis."

"Run into what?"

"Oh, small-mindedness." She shook her head. "Joyce won't let Brittany go with us to St. Clair's, and Marie is keeping Michaela home too."

"Why?"

"She made up some flimsy excuse, but the real reason is that some of those kids at St. Clair's have AIDS."

"You can't catch AIDS from giving a May basket to a sick kid," I said.

"I know that, you know that, and Joyce and Marie should know that too. I'm disappointed in both of them. It's just so narrow, so . . . so . . ."

"Stupid." I supplied a word my mother would never use when talking about another adult. She frowned slightly, but I knew it was the word she wanted.

Joyce Davis was not the only mom who called to cancel. By the time I'd put ribbons on all the May baskets, only four Sunbeams could make the trip, counting Vivian. Mom tried to be upbeat, but I could tell she was really bummed.

"I guess you were right," she said in this resigned, practical voice that didn't sound like her at all. "It wasn't such a good idea."

"No, it *is* a good idea," I said. "Those St. Clair kids *do* need to know people care. They do need to be around lively little girls like Vivian. And they'll like the flowers."

"Everyone likes flowers," Mom said absently. "But it's not much, really. Not much at all."

"It's something, though. It's a lot better than nothing!" I said, hoping she would believe I really meant it.

● ● ●

The next afternoon I helped Vivian and three other Sunbeams fill the take-out boxes with donated potted pansies, then loaded the Sunbeams and the May baskets

31

into Mom's van. The girls sang "The Ants Go Marching" all the way to St. Clair's, which was more than annoying, and Mom had regained her save-the-world energy. My own mood was less cheerful, to say the least.

When we got out of the van, Mom blew her silver scout-leader whistle. "You all know we're taking these baskets of flowers to children who are sick in the hospital. Why are we doing this?"

"To make them feel better," the Sunbeams chorused.

"Good. Now, some of these children will look different from you. Some will be very thin. Some will be in wheelchairs. Others may be bald."

I expected the Sunbeams to giggle, but they nodded solemnly, and I felt kind of proud of them.

"But they aren't different from you. They like to play and laugh and talk too. We don't want to stare at them. We don't want to make them feel embarrassed, do we?" The Sunbeams shook their heads. "Okay, each of you take two baskets, and Ginger and I will manage the rest."

We rode the elevator in silence, the girls looking up at themselves in the reflective metal walls until we reached the sixth floor. Reminding them to walk quietly, Mom led them to the pediatric ward. A nurse met us at the entrance.

"Good afternoon, girls," she said, bending and putting her hands on her knees so she could look each Sunbeam in the eye. "We're awfully glad you came to see us." She led them down the long hall to a room where about a dozen children were gathered. There were murals painted on the walls and yellow curtains on the windows. Some of the children were seated around board games; others drew with crayons or played with Lego's. When we entered, they stopped and looked at us. The Sunbeams huddled together just inside the door, staring wide-eyed around the room.

"You can go ahead in," the nurse said, and gently nudged Vivian and her friends into the room. Vivi stepped forward and handed her basket to a little girl with dark circles under her eyes and a bright pink kerchief covering her wispy hair.

"We made this just for you," Vivi said, and smiled her beautiful smile.

The little girl smiled back. "Want to play Candy Land?"

Soon the Sunbeams were scattered around the room playing games and building with Lego's. Some of the children looked pretty healthy; they might have been Sunbeams themselves, except they wore pajamas instead of yellow caps and blue vests. Others sat quietly watching, their faces pale and tired. It was hard to look at them, but impossible not to. How did that pediatric nurse stay so cheery all day long? How did the kids' parents stand it? How could you feel anything but helpless if you had to face these kids every day? But when a little boy walked up to me with a copy of *The Cat in the Hat,* I sat down with him and let him read it to me. What else could I do?

On the way home the Sunbeams talked in quiet voices about the children—Lisa, who got tired just playing Candy Land; Eric, who was in a wheelchair; Denita; Kristy; Rob.

"They don't seem very scared," Alex said. "Will they get better?"

"Some of them will," Mom said.

"What will happen to the ones who don't get better?" Vivian asked. "Will they die?"

"Sometimes children who are very sick do die," Mom answered in a firm voice. The Sunbeams were silent for a moment.

"They don't act afraid at all," Jaime said. "I would be scared if I was them."

"Maybe they are afraid. Maybe they just don't show it," Vivian said.

The Sunbeams fell silent, thinking about that until we got back to the Methodist church.

nicholas did call me again, just like he said he would, and by the time school was out in June we were what people at Cottonwood High consider a couple. I didn't consider us a couple, at least not the way Carter and Kim were—holding hands at lunch, leaving sappy notes in each other's lockers, and making out in the stairwell when no one was around. Sneaking around in stairwells and gazing at each other over plates of cafeteria food didn't strike me as anything but boring. At lunch I liked to eat fast and then go to the gym and shoot hoops until the bell rang for fourth period. Nicholas would be in the gym too sometimes, sometimes he wouldn't. It wasn't anything I counted on. Some days I had assignments to finish up in the library, and some days he'd be helping Mr. Withers work on the school Web site in the tech lab. If we ran into each other, fine; we'd shoot baskets and talk and kid around. If not, that was okay too.

He'd usually come by my locker before homeroom, but if he slipped anything in the little locker vents, it wouldn't be a sappy note. It would be a piece of gum or something he cut out of the newspaper, a cartoon or a funny article or just a goofy headline. Once it was this story about a girl who made her prom dress out of duct tape. No lie. She was hoping to win a hefty scholarship from the duct tape company—I don't know if she did or not. Another time it was an article on strange animal facts. Did you know that a tiger has striped skin, not just striped fur? Did you know that an ostrich's eye is bigger than its brain? That one kind of blew me away, for some reason. What a dumb animal. It's probably a good thing they can't fly. Well, that's the kind of thing Nicholas finds really interesting and likes to tell me about. Sometimes he'd stop me in the hall to tell me a joke that I wouldn't really get until he'd already walked off. Then I'd stand there laughing all by myself like some idiot, not caring who stared.

● ● ●

When school let out, Kim went off to this special camp for gifted kids she goes to for six weeks every summer. Camp Nerdland, she calls it, but she looks forward to it. Annie went to spend time with her dad in Denver. Her parents got divorced when we were in fifth grade, but she's still real close to her dad and spends at least a month with him every summer. He comes up here one weekend a month too, but Annie still complains about not seeing enough of him.

"So why don't you go live with him?" I asked her once. I guess it was kind of a mean thing to say to one of your best friends. Honestly, I'd hate for her to move away. But I was getting tired of her whining. At least she *sees* her dad. At least she knows who he is. Unlike me. Anyhow, that's where she was, doing all kinds of cool stuff in Denver while I was stuck in Cottonwood Falls.

Nicholas was the only person left to hang around with, so we got in the habit of shooting hoops in his driveway or, if I had to stick around home to take care of Vivian, sitting out on our deck playing games. He taught me and Vivian how to play dominoes, the regular kind as well as Chicken Foot and Mexican Train, but mostly we played cards. He knows all these games like Spite and Malice and pinochle, which I thought was strictly for senior citizens. If Mom and Tony weren't busy, they might sit in on a game of poker, which I was surprised to find out they both know how to play very well.

Sometimes we'd walk down to the Cuckoo's Nest, this coffee shop in Riverwood, a cool little area a mile or so from Curry Park. On one corner is the Diamond, this old movie theater, then the Video Barn, which has a great collection of classics. There's the Comix Shop and some hole-in-the-wall antiques stores. And the Cuckoo's Nest, a funky little place with local artists' work on the walls and live music on Friday nights. The owner, Mr. Roscoe, is a friend of the Blackstones, and Nicholas was hoping to get

37

a job there over the summer. Secretly I was hoping he wouldn't for two reasons, both completely selfish. First, I wouldn't be able to see as much of him, and second, Mandy Roscoe. Mandy is the owner's daughter, a bouncy blond junior who clearly has the hots for Nicholas. Every time we'd go in there, she'd give him a big friend-of-the-family hug and jump around and giggle a lot. Then she'd say hello to me like I was about as welcome as salmonella.

"You'd think Mandy would get tired of the same old routine," I said one afternoon as we browsed through the latest editions in the Comix Shop.

"What do you mean?"

"That huggy thing she does. Is she always so physical?"

"That's just Mandy. You don't need to worry about her."

"Who's worried?" I asked, and Nicholas grinned. It wasn't that I didn't want Nicholas to be friends with other girls, but there was something about Mandy's bounciness that really got on my nerves. Still, the Nest was the only place to go, Mandy or no Mandy.

On warm afternoons when Mom didn't need me to baby-sit, Nicholas and I would bike out to Moose Lake, about seven miles south of town. We'd pack up chips and soda, a deck of cards, and this old transistor radio in a black leather case that Nicholas inherited from his dad. We both liked the radio better than a CD player. For one thing, you didn't have to carry around a bunch of discs. And we could turn it to whatever we were in the mood for. Sometimes we'd even listen to talk radio and laugh at the silly things adults get steamed about. After the sun baked us good and hot, we'd swim out to the wooden raft floating a ways offshore. We'd lie there warming up, wishing we didn't have to get back into the cold water again, until late in the afternoon. And we'd talk. That's the thing I like most about Nicholas, the way I can talk to him about anything. Not just personal stuff like Vivian getting on my nerves or Mom always missing the point—which I talked about plenty—but all kinds of stuff.

"Did you know there are one million nurdles per mile on some California beaches?" He'd start with something like that, something that came from way outside the normal conversation zone.

"What's a nurdle?" I asked, and he told me about the tiny bits of plastic garbage replacing the sand on our beaches, about the one thousand shipping containers that fall off boats each year, spilling everything from Nikes to rubber ducks to fresh produce. Did you know oranges distribute themselves like oil spills? A million floating oranges once provided a great learning tool for ecologists. Sometimes we'd talk about the possibility of life on other planets or where you go when you die or what lucky accident occurred to get us born in this century instead of the 1400s or here instead of some Third World country. These were topics that Nicholas brought up, stuff I'd kind of vaguely considered but never really put into words. Okay, it's weird stuff. Still, after a while I couldn't remember why I had once thought Nicholas himself was so weird.

•   •   •

One afternoon we were over at his house shooting baskets when his dad came out on the porch and announced he was cooking Thai and asked if I would like to stay for dinner. I wasn't sure what cooking Thai was (cooking tie?), but I said sure, I'd call and see if it was all right with my parents. When I went into the Blackstones' house to use the phone, I couldn't get over the smell of whatever Mr. Blackstone had on the stove. It was really wonderful—kind of smoky-spicy, like nothing I'd ever smelled in my kitchen. Not even Tony's famous Tijuana chicken wings, which, as he says, will put hair on your chest, could match whatever was in Mr. Blackstone's wok.

"I'll try not to add too much fire," Mr. Blackstone said when I got off the phone. I smiled. I thought I knew spicy, but I didn't have a clue what he was talking about until I took a bite of thom yum goong and felt my head about to erupt.

"Give Ginger more water, Nicholas," Mr. Blackstone said, his eyes sparkling mischievously. For a minute I could vividly imagine him at age twelve putting hand lotion on doorknobs, short-sheeting beds, filling water balloons. He was eating the stuff like it was popcorn.

"I should have warned you," Nicholas said. "But he always gets a kick out of that first reaction. You should have seen Carter. I thought we'd have to dial 911." I was sucking down glass after glass of water, my eyes tearing up. "The other dishes aren't nearly so bad, I promise."

He was right. The dinner was the best. And the dessert, a white chocolate mousse drizzled with raspberry sauce, was absolutely to die for.

Everything about Nicholas's parents and their house is completely different from mine. Dinner—the food, the crystal, the china, the cloth napkins—was just a start. The Blackstones' house is big and rambling, with lots of exposed wood and stone. Mine is cramped and cluttered, with lots of carpet and linoleum. Then there's this grand piano in the living room stacked with sheet music and books and a bust of Mozart. There's hardly an inch of wall space that isn't covered with art—not those pictures that you buy at Pier I to go with the furniture, but real black-and-white photographs, a huge pastel portrait of Nicholas at about five years old, antique maps. There are oriental rugs and shelves full of books and a sunroom so crammed with orchids you can hardly get in there. It isn't something out of *Martha Stewart Living*, but the house has a sense of order to it, a feeling of harmony.

Mr. Blackstone is a lawyer and is kind of handsome in an elegant way. I wouldn't be surprised if he had a tuxedo somewhere in his closet, one he actually wears. Mrs. Blackstone is really beautiful, even though she's pushing fifty, tall and willowy with silvery blond hair that she wears in a loose bun and skin that looks like it never saw the sun. She's incredibly pale, but it looks great on her. She used to play piano professionally until she broke her hand skiing in Switzerland. Now she gives lessons, mostly to St. Sebastian students.

After dinner Nicholas walked me home through Curry Park. It was still light out, even though it was after nine o'clock. Swallows were skimming the surface of the pond, meeting their wavery shadows on the water in a quick kiss. The half-moon hung in the deep blue sky while its twin shone up from the still water.

"Two worlds," Nicholas said. "One up, one down." I nodded, thinking how strange it was to know exactly what he was talking about. He took my hand and then he

chapter 5

after the trip to St. Clair's a couple of the Sunbeams dropped out for good. At first Mom was on the phone with their mothers, trying to convince them that seven years old is not too young for children to understand what she called their relationship with the larger community, but the other moms didn't see it that way. After a while she just gave up.

Frankly, I could see their point.

"Were you active in your community at age seven?" I asked, knowing this was a risky question.

"Was I active?" She fluffed her hair and I steeled myself for a verbal barrage. "Was I active?" she repeated in a different tone of voice, and sighed. "No. At seven I was a holy terror and a good candidate for Most Selfish Child on the Planet. Plus, my parents would never have allowed me to associate with *those people*. The ones who might need help."

I nodded.

"But it would have done me a world of good. If I'd seen more at seven, I might have been better at seventeen."

Maybe we'd do normal Sunbeam Scout things now, I thought, like make papier-maché boxes or macaroni necklaces. After one meeting when we painted T-shirts and a good portion of the Methodists' basement floor, I had an even better idea: maybe we could just shut down for the summer. "Isn't that what most scout troops do?" I asked Mom. "Isn't there a rule somewhere about not meeting during summer vacation?" But Mom only gave me that Disappointed Mother look and took out the *Sunbeam Leader Guide* to try to get more ideas. Unfortunately there was nothing in the guide that looked worthwhile. Instead, Mom got her next idea from the *Cottonwood Daily Chronicle*.

It was Sunday morning, and Tony had just served up some of his secret-recipe blueberry waffles with warm syrup. Vivian was in her pajamas reading the comics, Tony had the sports section, and Mom, still in her robe, was looking at the living section. At that exact moment we looked like a perfectly normal family—waffles, coffee cups, Sunday paper—and then Mom saw the ad.

"Hey, listen to this," she said. " 'Servers needed at the Rescue Bowl. All volunteers welcome.' "

"The which bowl?" Tony asked, peering over the sports pages. Apparently he thought she was talking about football.

"The Rescue Bowl. It's an emergency food dispensary. A soup kitchen."

"Where is it located?" Tony asked, pouring syrup all over his bacon and eggs as well as his waffles, something I can hardly stand to witness without feeling barfy, although I've seen him do it for years.

"Down on Second and Monterey," Mom said.

"Not the most scenic part of town."

"Of course not. It's a soup kitchen."

"Isn't that biker place down there?" Tony asked. "Harleys for Jesus?"

"Are you referring to the Bikers' Evangelical Mission?" Mom asked in a voice that could cool the waffles and the coffee too. "I have no problem with evangelical missions as long as they help people out and don't proselytize."

Isn't proselytizing the main thing evangelicals do? I almost asked.

"Renee, it's not the evangelicals I have a problem with, it's the bikers," Tony said. "Don't you want to keep *any* of the Sunbeams?"

"Don't you want Vivi to keep any of her *friends,* is the question," I said, which was a mistake, because then Mom directed her tirade about helping others at me, not Tony. Luckily, it was a short tirade. Despite Tony's reservations, Mom gave the Rescue Bowl a call and set a date for the Sunbeams to serve up some plates.

"It's only this once," she assured Tony. "Besides, it's a family place, single moms and the elderly, mostly. No alcohol or drug use allowed. It's a perfectly safe place for the girls."

"If you insist on going, I'll go with you," Tony said.

"Now how are you going to do that with work behind schedule and Tim laid up with his back? Don't worry about us. We'll have fun. If we run into any trouble, we'll call in the evangelical bikers."

"Very funny, Renee. I'd feel better if it weren't just you and a bunch of little girls."

"Ginger will be there."

I could tell Tony had included me under the heading "little girls," but he wasn't going to say so in front of me.

"Okay, okay." Mom sighed. "I'll get Suzanne to go with us." Then she turned to me. "And maybe Nick would like to help out." Mom is the only person I know who calls Nicholas Nick. Nobody, not even his own mother, calls him that. But he doesn't seem to mind. He and my mother get along incredibly well. Mainly because they're both such idealists. As soon as Nicholas heard about Mom's lofty ideas for the Sunbeams, he decided she could do no wrong, and that, of course, made him almost infallible in her eyes, as well. I couldn't tell what Tony thought of him. Most of the time they just said hello in these manly voices and traded a sentence or two about sports.

Tony finally agreed to let us go, and Suzanne said she'd be glad to help out. I decided to simply forget to mention the Rescue Bowl to Nicholas, but when he came over that afternoon with his box of dominoes, Mom jumped on him first thing. I wasn't at all surprised when he said okay. In fact, he'd volunteered there last summer and said the director, Cathy, was cool.

"It'll be a great place to take the kids," he said.

"Wonderful. You make it sound like a theme park," I said.

"What's wrong with letting kids see a little of the world around them?" he asked. "They need to see life is more than Barbies and Pokémon."

"Pokémon's out."

"Okay, Beanie Babies. Whatever."

It wasn't something I wanted to spend the afternoon discussing, so I challenged him to a game of Chicken Foot. Nicholas really takes competition seriously. He frowns through the whole game, even when he's winning, all his energy concentrated on strategy. He's not a sore loser, but he's a terrible winner who won't let you forget your mistakes. For a guy who is pretty casual and open-minded about other things, he's a regular tyrant with a box of dominoes. I like to play, but winning isn't that big a deal with me, so I usually end up laughing at him, win or lose, for being overly intense. It's a pretty good combination. Even when we're on opposing sides, we make a good team.

● ● ●

On Tuesday afternoon Nicholas and I helped Mom pile the remaining Sunbeams into the van, and we headed for the Rescue Bowl. It's located in what used to be a small elementary school near the freeway. Before the freeway was built thirty years ago, this was one of the oldest neighborhoods in Cottonwood Falls, Mom said as we drove along. Then the highway department condemned two dozen residential blocks, bused the students somewhere else, and paved a six-lane with on-ramps. What's left of the old neighborhood isn't much to look at: big wooden houses with gingerbread trim falling off the eaves, scrubby beige grass, and big dogs behind chain-link fences. Not the kind of neighborhood many people would want to live in, including the people who live there. But what else can they do? The houses are mostly rental property now, Mom said. The landlords are notorious for neglect and unfair pricing. And why should the tenants care about paint and landscaping when fifty yards away they have constant traffic kicking up dust and making a racket?

"It's a shame," Mom said, shaking her head.

Nicholas agreed, and they discussed the problem of urban decay until we took the Monterey Street exit and drove up to the Rescue Bowl.

Suzanne's red convertible was in the parking lot, and she was already inside talking to the director, Cathy Andrews. When Cathy saw Nicholas, she gave him a big hug.

"Hey there, Stringbean," Suzanne said. "Nicholas, have they made you an official Sunbeam big brother or what?"

"I, Nicholas, promise to do my best. . . ."

"Are you talking Sunbeam?" Suzanne laughed.

"Cub Scouts. But I only made it to Wolf, then dropped out. I couldn't stand those kerchief things."

There were people milling around waiting to line up, and a few kids were running around the tables while their moms acted like they belonged to someone else. I don't know what I was expecting—abject poverty, maybe—but most of the people seemed pretty average, except their clothes looked secondhand and the kids' hair needed combing. In all fairness, though, a couple of the Sunbeams could have used a comb too, and so could Nicholas, who was a frequent Goodwill shopper himself. So what was the difference really, except he could choose whether to wear thrift-shop clothes and the kids and moms in line couldn't? Poverty doesn't always look like what you would expect, Mom said earlier that day in one of her mini sermons. Now I understood what she meant. There were a lot of elderly people, some quite dignified-looking, like they'd only recently fallen on hard times. A couple of young guys smoked just outside the door. They looked like they didn't much want to be there, but they got in line anyway.

Cathy gave Vivi and the other Sunbeams clear plastic gloves and put them in charge of handing out rolls. The rest of us spooned up green beans and potatoes and meat loaf, which looked pretty good, though I don't know how it tasted. We weren't quite finished serving when Mom decided she'd take the girls home. It was after seven, and she'd promised to have them home by seven-thirty. Suzanne, Nicholas, and I stayed to help Cathy clean up and shut down.

Right after Mom left, the man came in.

I guess I noticed him first because he got there so late and he was so tall. Nicholas was bagging up the extra rolls and Suzanne was asking Cathy what to do with the leftover meat loaf when he came up to get a plate. Cathy looked at her watch, then nodded to him that it was okay to go through the line, but you could tell she wished he'd come in earlier. Only an old man and his wife, who was in a wheelchair, were left sitting at a table.

"You'll have to make it quick," Cathy said, looking at him closely, maybe to make sure he wasn't drunk, which is one of the rules at the Rescue Bowl. I looked at him carefully too. He was tall, like I said, and had a blond ponytail.

I guess he was about forty, and he didn't look as down on his luck as a lot of the folks we'd served. He had on nice jeans and a brown suede jacket, though it was a warm night, and he carried what looked like a camera bag slung over his shoulder. Around his left wrist he wore a silver-and-turquoise bracelet engraved with an intricate Southwest Indian design. He must have felt me looking at him because before he picked up his plate, he gazed straight at me with ice blue eyes. I thought for a minute he was going to say something, but then Nicholas held out a spoonful of mashed potatoes.

"Here you go, sir," he said, and the man kind of blinked like he was coming out of a trance and finally picked up a plate. Maybe he was a little unbalanced or a little strung out. Maybe he was just tired. At any rate, there was something about him that made me nervous. At the same time, I felt like I'd seen him somewhere before, like he was on the verge of telling me where, when Nicholas spooned up the potatoes and he went on down the line and over to the farthest table. He sat with his back to us, hunkered down over his plate.

I helped Nicholas and Cathy carry leftovers back into the kitchen, and when we returned to the serving line, the man was gone.

"Whoa, talk about scarfing up your dinner," Nicholas said.

"He seemed a little odd, didn't he?"

"He probably *is* a little odd."

"Did you see the way he stared at us?" I didn't want to say stared at *me*. I didn't want to sound paranoid.

"Did he?" Nicholas asked. "I didn't really notice."

I told myself there could be lots of reasons why he stood there like he wanted to say something to me. Maybe he was about to ask for extra rolls or wanted to tell us to hold the beans. Maybe he was about to say thank you. Forget it, I told myself. And maybe I would have if I hadn't seen him again just a couple of days later.

I had taken Vivian down to Curry Park to play on the swings while I messed around on the basketball court next to the playground. I had asked Nicholas to meet us there, but he had to work. He'd finally gotten a job busing tables at the Cuckoo's Nest. Since he'd wanted the job so badly, I was glad for him, but I really missed spending time with him. And there was bouncy Mandy, who I tried to not think about. Anyway, there I was working on my outside shot, which needs major work, and Vivi was swinging too high—you can't tell her a thing—and singing to herself. One mom and a couple of toddlers were there at first, but they left after a while, so it was just the two of us. Or that's what I thought until all of a sudden I saw this guy sitting on top of the big slide, backward, his feet on the top rung. He was facing the swings and kind of smiling at Vivi.

At first I thought he was some high school kid because of the way he was dressed and his long hair and red bandana, but then he looked directly at me with those ice blue eyes and I recognized him. He was the guy from the Rescue Bowl and, it finally dawned on me, the guy who had been staring at me and Kim and Annie jogging through the park. That had been weeks earlier, but it came back to me clearly, the way his head had moved like some kind of tracking device. I felt this rush through my body and threw a wild shot that went over the backboard, and for a minute I panicked, afraid to go get the ball because there he was watching Vivi again. But then I told myself I was being ridiculous and sprinted after the ball anyway. Vivi was still having a blast sailing back and forth, singing every song she knows, but I went over to her and told her it was time to go. Of course she put up a fuss, claiming that we hadn't been there long enough, that she'd be bored at home, that I'd promised to stay until she said, which wasn't true. Luckily I heard the ice cream truck about a block away.

"I'll buy you a Creamsicle," I said, and she flew off the swing like a trapeze artist, perfect landing and all, and we got the hell out of there. I couldn't help looking back just in time to see him gliding down the slide. I was afraid he might follow us, but he just sat there at the bottom of the slide, staring after us as we left the park. He had this enigmatic smile on his face, and even at that distance, I swear I saw him wink.

•   •   •

When we got home, Mom was putting away groceries in the kitchen. After two nights of SpaghettiOs for dinner she'd finally made it to the store. "Who'd you see at the park?" she asked Vivi.

"Some little kids. Nobody I know," Vivi said. "Ginger made me leave early, but then she got me a Creamsicle."

"Well, that was nice of you, Ginger. I'll pay you back."

"It's okay," I said. The tall man didn't seem all that important now that we were back in our own kitchen watching Mom stack boxes of frozen vegetables in the freezer.

So I didn't mention him. In fact, I was a little embarrassed about how he had creeped me out. Still, I was sure he was the same guy we'd served meat loaf and potatoes to and who I'd seen sitting on a picnic table by the duck pond. What he was doing in Curry Park, so far from the Rescue Bowl, was a mystery to me. Still, it's a free country. Like Mom said, he's got a right to be there.

• • •

That night I got a call from Annie. She'd been in Denver for over a week and was having a great time with her dad, hiking and eating out and shopping for stereo equipment. And then there was the boy next door.

"He's absolutely adorable," she cooed. "Kind of Elijah Wood–ish."

"You mean like a hobbit?"

"No, not the Frodo Elijah, the normal one. And he drives," she added.

"Your dad lets you ride around with him?"

"Yeah, but mostly we just hang out at his pool," she said, and paused to let that sink in. "So how are things going in good ol' Cottonwood Falls?"

"As thrilling as ever." I told her about Nicholas's job, which was the most exciting development in my life, I realized with dismay. "Hey, you remember that guy who was staring at us at the park that day we were running?" I asked.

"Which guy?"

"You know, the creepy older guy!"

"Creepy older guy . . ."

"With the suede jacket and bandana?"

"I don't remem— Oh yeah. The guy *you* saw. I didn't really notice him. So what about him?"

"I don't know," I mumbled. What could I say? Seeing a strange man whose name I didn't know wasn't much news. Why had I even brought it up?

"Hey, I've got to run. Devon's here. Can I call you back later? Say hi to Nicholas, okay?" I could almost feel the breeze she created dashing out the door and into Devon's car.

The fact that Annie hadn't remembered the tall guy made me wonder why he was making such an impression on me. It wasn't just because I'd seen him a couple more times than she had. It was like I was supposed to know him from somewhere. Like I had known him in a former life, Nicholas might say. But I didn't really believe in reincarnation. Something else was going on.

●   ●   ●

It wasn't until the fourth time I saw the tall guy that I figured it out. Nicholas and I were in the Video Barn looking for Marx Brothers movies. I'd never seen one. They're not the kind of thing my family watches on Friday nights. Tony is big on martial arts and police thrillers, and Mom watches whatever is newly released and then promptly forgets everything about it. Was that the one with the girl he drowned and her ghost comes back? she'll ask. Was that the one where they wear those revealing space suits? Vivian was with us, clutching a copy of *Lilo & Stitch*, which she's seen about fifteen times already but just had to watch again. Unlike Mom, Vivian memorizes movies.

She knows this one so well she can recite it practically line for line. We were standing at the checkout with *A Night at the Opera* and *Lilo & Stitch* when the tall guy came through the door. I nudged Nicholas with my toe and nodded toward him.

"What?" Nicholas said, and Vivi looked up at me expectantly. She rarely misses a thing.

"Remember him?" I said in a low voice, trying not to move my lips.

"That's the guy from the Rescue Bowl, isn't it?" Nicholas said a little too loudly, but I was glad he recognized him right off because then I knew it wasn't just me being paranoid. The guy circled the store a couple of times. He didn't seem to be looking for anything in particular. In fact, he hardly seemed to be looking at the videos at all. We rented our movies and left while he was in the Horror section.

"I think he's following me," I said as we crossed the street.

"Who is?" Vivian asked, but I ignored her.

"Why do you think that?" Nicholas asked.

"Did he seem to be interested in finding a video to you?"

"He's probably waiting until the place clears out so he can rent something from the adult section without being embarrassed." The Video Barn has a back room curtained off with heavy black velvet that you can't enter unless you're eighteen.

"Yeah, right. Besides, I've seen him another time." I told Nicholas about him being at the playground the day before.

"Just a coincidence. Maybe he lives in the neighborhood."

"And eats at the Rescue Bowl?"

"Maybe he's just eccentric."

"What's *eccentric* mean?" asked Vivi.

"Strange," I told her. "It's more than a coincidence," I said to Nicholas, then told him about the first time he had shown up in Curry Park.

"You don't think he's stalking you or something, do you?" Nicholas asked in a tone of voice I didn't like at all.

"I didn't say *stalking*." We stopped at the corner and looked back at the Video Barn. We hadn't been out of the store for two minutes, and there he was, standing just outside the door, looking around. Nicholas pulled me and Vivian behind an SUV, and we watched him trying to decide which way to go. He took a camera with a telephoto lens out of his bag and scanned the street.

"What's he doing?" I whispered. "Looking for us?"

"Who is?" Vivian asked.

"Okay, let's be logical here." Nicholas's voice was kind of breathless and he was talking fast. "Say he is looking for you. Why would he be doing that? Maybe he thinks he knows you. Are you sure you've never seen him before?"

"Not until just recently," I said. I didn't want to tell Nicholas the tall guy somehow looked familiar. He'd think I'd completely lost it.

"Maybe he's got you mixed up with somebody else."

"Great, what am I supposed to do about that?" I asked.

"For one thing, we could just go up and start talking to him."

"And say what? 'Hi, you don't know me, but you think you do'?"

"We'll just ask him if he's looking for someone. Come on. We should be direct about this."

"I'll ask him," said Vivi.

"You don't even know what we're talking about," I said.

"I do too. You're talking about that man with the red bandana. That man we saw at the park yesterday. And I saw him drive by our house yesterday too. He waved to me."

Nicholas and I looked at each other, then back at the tall guy. There was something about him, something familiar. . . .

Then all of a sudden it hit me. My stomach felt like a Slinky that had just spilled to the ground and sprung up again. My knees felt like Slinkies too, all stretchy-wobbly, but I grabbed Vivian and started walking as fast as I could down a side street, away from the tall guy and the Video Barn.

Nicholas ran up behind us. "What's going on?"

I know who he is, I mouthed over Vivian's head so she wouldn't hear me.

Who? Nicholas mouthed back.

I looked down at Vivi walking between us, jumping over cracks in the sidewalk, then at Nicholas.

My father.

chapter 6

"are you sure about this?" Nicholas asked when we got home. We were sitting on the deck. Vivian was inside watching her movie, so we could finally talk in private. Nicholas knew Tony was my stepdad—anybody could tell at first glance we weren't related—but he didn't know the details about my real dad. Even I didn't know the details, but I knew I was right about the tall guy.

"Wouldn't you know your own father?" I asked.

"Of course," Nicholas said, "but I live with the man. How long has it been since you last saw yours?"

The fact was that I hadn't seen him since I was three years old, and then only for a visit I don't even remember.

Mom just told me about it later. When I was twelve, she got a bunch of pictures together to show me who my real father was and tell me a little bit about him. She said his name was Austin Trantor and they had met in college. He was tall and played basketball. That was about it. This revelation occurred right after she read a magazine article about this girl who sued her mother for keeping her biological father's identity a secret. He was some wealthy software mogul, and here this girl had been living in a trailer park in Idaho while he'd been trying to locate her. The girl won the lawsuit and now lives with her dad in a mansion in California, as I recall. Mom hadn't mentioned my dad since then.

"You don't forget someone like your own father," I told Nicholas, who shrugged.

Mom came out on the deck with a bowl of strawberries. "These berries are one hundred percent organic," she said. "Eat all you want, there are more in the fridge. I'm going to take Vivian to look for some new sandals. Hers are so small her toes hang over the edge. I'll be back in an hour or so. Need anything while I'm out?"

"No. Thanks," I said, impatient for her to leave.

"Remember the rules," she reminded me as she closed the door. There are several rules at our house, but the one she was referring to specifically was the No Young Men Allowed in the House Without Parental Supervision rule. Nicholas and I could stay out on the deck, but he was not allowed inside unless she or Tony was at home. Still, I figured we had at least an hour, and there was something in the basement he just had to help me find.

"You sure this is okay?" Nicholas asked as I led him

into the house and down the stairs. He'd never been in the basement before, since it includes only my bedroom—always off limits—a bathroom, the computer, and some storage areas. "Wow, this is so cool. You've got all this space," he said, poking his head in the partially finished rooms along the hallway. For years Tony's been planning to get to them as soon as he has time.

"It's not really mine. Most of it's full of my mom's junk." We went into a room with roughed-out walls and a bare bulb overhead. You could hardly see the gray vinyl flooring for all the stuff crammed in there. Cardboard boxes stacked three or four tall, two or three deep. Plastic garbage bags of craft materials that the Sunbeams would never use and Mom would never throw out. Extra furniture.

"What I'm looking for is this box of old pictures and yearbooks and stuff," I explained as I shoved boxes around. "I know it's down here."

"It would help if this stuff were labeled," Nicholas said. I had a sudden vision of the Blackstones' basement: sturdy matching boxes made especially for storage with little metal label holders and labels printed in calligraphy. Boxes filled with valuable heirlooms, not worthless junk.

"Whoa, look at this. A Mystery Date game. And look at these Archie comics. These are collector's items."

"You're supposed to be helping me," I said, rummaging through boxes of baby clothes, picture books, kitchen stuff, a set of black dishes that Tony brought with him when he and Mom got married. I remember the dishes well because one night at dinner, Mom said they were funereal, and we never used them again. Tony just packed them up and put them away, which at the time I thought was very considerate. Looking back on it now, I think he might have been irritated or even hurt by Mom's tactlessness. Still, I have to admit they are pretty hideous. With my luck, I'll inherit them one day.

"Here we go. This is what you're looking for." Nicholas held up a large blue book with raised gold lettering on the cover. "Middlebrook College, 1987?"

"Let me see." Nicholas handed it to me and I opened it to the junior class pictures. "Trantor, Trantor," I murmured. "Austin Trantor." My hands were trembly and my stomach was threatening to become a Slinky again as I turned the page and found it: my dad's class picture in living color.

"That's him?" Nicholas said, leaning over my shoulder, so close I could feel his breath on my cheek.

"Yep." We looked at Austin Trantor, twenty years old, with spiky hair, a long nose, and a mischievous mouth. A pair of sunglasses, classic Ray•Bans, covered his eyes. "Do you think it's the tall guy?" I asked, though I had no doubt in my mind.

"It does look like him," he said, "but the picture's so small, and with the sunglasses it's hard to tell. Is there a larger one somewhere?"

I flipped to the sports section and found a full-page color shot of the basketball team. There he was, A. Trantor, number thirty-seven. He was standing in the back row. His chin was hidden by the guy in front of him, but his eyes were clear, pale blue. It was the tall guy for sure. That was my dad we'd served at the Rescue Bowl. That was my dad at Curry Park and at the Video Barn. For a second, I thought I would burst into tears. Don't ask me

why. Out of relief, out of disappointment, out of pure excitement—I really don't know.

"What do I do now?" I asked Nicholas, trying to pull
myself together.

"Nothing. Wait. See what he's going to do first, maybe.
He must know who you are if he's your dad. That's why
he's here in Cottonwood Falls, right? He must want to get
in touch with you. If it's him."

"Then why doesn't he just do it?" I said, ignoring his
last point.

"He's probably got his reasons."

"I wonder if he's tried to get in touch with Mom."

Just then, we heard the garage door opening over our
heads. "I guess you can ask her when she comes in and
finds us," Nicholas said, looking trapped. "Is there any
other way out of here?"

"Only those stairs we came down," I whispered, and
put a hand up to his mouth. "Just be quiet."

"Gin, are you down there?" Mom called from the top
of the stairs. I shooed Nicholas into the bathroom. "Is that
Nick's bike in the front yard?"

"In our yard? Oh yeah," I called up to her.

"Well, where's Nick?"

"What?" I called, standing in front of the bathroom door.

"I said, where is Nicholas?" She was starting down the
stairs.

"He's gone. Just a sec and I'll be right up. I've really
got to go to the bathroom." Mom turned and went back
upstairs.

"Just get in the bathtub, behind the shower curtain," I
whispered to Nicholas. "I'll get you out in a little while." I

flushed the toilet and ran the water in the sink for a few seconds, then turned out the light.

"It's pitch-black in here," Nicholas muttered. "How am I supposed to see?"

"You don't need to see. Just be quiet. She'll go into her bedroom or something in a minute and I'll be able to sneak you out." I climbed the stairs trying to think of reasons why Nicholas's bike would be in the front yard if Nicholas himself was somewhere else, trying to think of where that somewhere else might be.

It wasn't until I got started talking that the story developed. Carter had just gotten his driver's license, which was true. And he had come by to pick up Nicholas for a ride, which was not true. They were going to the music store, I said, and then stopped myself before I went into too much detail. If you're going to lie, keep it simple, says Kim, who lies to her parents more than I like to admit. It was taking forever for Mom to get out of the kitchen. I was so busy keeping an eye on her that I forgot about Vivi until I heard her scream.

Mom took off down the basement stairs to see what the problem was. I was right behind her. I knew exactly what the problem was, and I wished Vivi would stop screaming. After the first shock of finding Nicholas in the bathtub, she should have been all right. Of course, maybe she was just enjoying herself, screaming at the top of her lungs, playing the drama queen, as usual. Maybe she thought she was being funny. Then I saw Nicholas sitting in the tub holding his hand up to his bloody face and I nearly screamed myself. He'd stumbled over Vivian's tub toys and hit the faucet on the way down.

"I was just looking for my mermaid Barbie and I heard something fall down in the bathtub and when I opened the shower curtain it was Nicholas and he's all bloody and gross." She covered her eyes.

"Are you all right?" Mom wet a bath towel and dabbed Nicholas's face. "Does it hurt?"

"I'm okay," Nicholas said, taking the white towel and wiping an amazing amount of blood from what was really a very tiny cut on his upper lip. "And I can explain everything."

I truly believe that if he hadn't said that, Mom would have forgotten to get mad at us for breaking the No Young Men rule in the first place. Instead, she pulled her shoulders back and asked, "What is the meaning of this?" in such a phony-sounding voice that I almost laughed, even though she was absolutely serious.

"I can explain," Nicholas said again, but I shook my head at him. Mom was fluffing her hair, hyper-fluffing, in overdrive. It would be much better to just let her blow off steam. We had broken the rule, after all. Why wasn't important. And I wasn't at all sure what Nicholas might say. I didn't really want to announce that my father was in town looking for me. So there we stood, Nicholas still in the bathtub with a damp towel turning pink against his lip, Mom going on and on about responsibility and trust and making good choices, and me nearly dying of embarrassment. She knew we hadn't been doing anything seriously bad down there, I mean like having sex or doing drugs, but she is a big one for rules. Plus, she reminded me after Nicholas left, I had lied to her. That was the biggest disappointment of all.

chapter 7

i was grounded for three weeks. For three weeks I wasn't allowed to see Nicholas or even go out of the house without a specific reason, like taking Vivi to the park or attending a Sunbeam meeting. For three weeks I had to limit my phone calls to five minutes each. Even Tony thought the phone restriction was a little extreme, but he knew better than to interfere with Mom and the rules. Disciplining me was her department.

A couple of days after I got grounded, Annie called.

"You can only talk for five minutes?" she asked in disbelief when I told her the situation. "But I've got so much to tell you! Devon and I went to the Miskommunikation concert. Can you believe it? And tomorrow my dad and I are going to a dude ranch for a couple of days. When we get back, Devon's having a big pool party with a DJ and everything." I let her go on for four more minutes until Mom pointed at the clock.

"E-mail me," I said, and hung up.

Kim was still at camp, and I got a lengthy e-mail from her once a week. The Nerdland News, she called it, but she was having a great time. At least the computer wasn't off limits. I wrote them both a long letter about finding Austin Trantor, but then deleted it without hitting Send. I wasn't sure how much I wanted Kim and Annie to know, not yet anyway. Not until I knew how things were going to turn out. Annie might understand, since her parents are divorced. But her situation is so normal, nothing like being the daughter of some mystery man who eats at soup kitchens and hangs out in public parks. And Kim would never understand. Her parents were high school sweethearts. Her whole extended family lives within a fifteen-mile radius. Only Nicholas knew what was going on. But he wasn't calling.

● ● ●

It took two whole days after I'd been grounded before Mom and I finally had a real conversation. Up until then I'd mainly been lectured to death. Vivian was over at her friend Alex's house, and Tony was at work. Mom had enlisted me to help her clean out the kitchen cabinets as an excuse to have me in the same room with her. I guess she was hoping for some mother-daughter interaction, but nothing was happening. The radio was turned to an oldies station, and except for every now and then when she sang along for a couple of lines, nobody said anything. As a rule I don't listen to oldies. It's just not my kind of music. Of course, it's not Mom's kind of music either, technically. She ought to be listening to disco or punk or whatever they were listening to twenty years ago. It's weird, but all the parents I know just turn the dial to oldies, like after you turn thirty you might as well be fifty. Anyway, Mom was singing along to some song about this birthday girl crying because her boyfriend dumped her for a girl named Judy. She was standing on a chair handing me some Tupperware when all of a sudden she stopped singing and asked if I knew why I was grounded.

At first I thought, This is a trick question, and didn't know how to answer, but she asked again, louder, like she thought I was ignoring her.

"Because I lied," I told her.

Mom studied me. "Ginger, do you need to be considering some sort of birth control?"

I nearly dropped the tower of Tupperware. I could feel my face turn all red, and I was afraid she'd take that to mean I do need birth control, which I don't. I couldn't believe she asked me something like that. I couldn't believe she might think I'm *sexually active,* which is the phrase all the teachers use beginning about fifth grade when they deliver those embarrassing human growth and development lectures. I mean, I know people my age are doing it. I know statistics even suggest I could be one of them, but I'm not, and I told her so.

"Don't act so shocked," she said, and fluffed her

bangs. "I was sexually active"—I couldn't believe she used that phrase—"by the time I got my driver's license."

My mother's past was not something I wanted to hear about, but she kept talking.

"I was one of those girls who didn't have a very good reputation in high school. To be perfectly honest," she said, and I felt like telling her not to be, "it's a miracle you don't have any older siblings."

"I guess you were just lucky until I came along," I said.

That shut her up for a minute, and me too, since I couldn't believe I said it. Then she asked, "Do you believe that?"

When I didn't say anything, she climbed off the chair she'd been standing on and sat me down at the kitchen table. She sat across from me and stared at me with teary-looking eyes. "Do you really believe that? Because if you do, you've got everything wrong." She put her hand on mine. "You are the best thing that ever happened to me, Ginger. Don't you ever think anything different. You changed my life in ways I never would have imagined fifteen years ago." Then she told me all this stuff I wasn't so sure I wanted to hear, like how she didn't get along with her parents and skipped school and made bad grades and the wrong kind of friends.

"Suzanne always looked out for me. I guess thanks to me, she got an early education on what not to do. It's a wonder she still speaks to me after some of the stuff I put her through." She shook her head. "Did you know your grandfather never really forgave me? When he died, we hadn't spoken to each other for five years. It was really hard on him, my having a baby, not finishing college and all that. The thing I regret most is not making up with him before it was too late."

"When was the last time you talked to *my* dad?" I asked, trying to keep it casual.

"Your dad?"

"Austin," I said, but it came out in a hoarse whisper, so I cleared my throat and tried again. "Austin Trantor."

"A long time ago." She began nesting plastic bowls one inside the other, then taking them out, then nesting them again. "Your father was—let's see, what would you call him now? A dude? A slacker?" She looked at me to see if those terms in any way registered. I shrugged, but I got her point.

"He came from a very well-to-do family from Tacoma and had a lot of things, a lot of opportunities. But he could never focus."

"When did you meet him?" I asked.

"Sophomore year at Middlebrook. He led the basketball team to the conference championship. He was a great athlete." She paused. "That's where you get it, you know, Ginger, the height and the great ball handling."

I'm mediocre, like I said, but I accepted the compliment. I knew she was trying to smooth things over between us.

"Anyway, that didn't last. Right after the championship he got kicked off the team for smoking dope. Which he was also selling. That and other things. I didn't know all this at the time—nobody knew all of it—but I doubt it would have made any difference to me. I was smitten. Exactly why, I can't recall." She capped the nest of Tupperware with a plastic top. "I don't mean to paint

69

your father as a bad person, Ginger. I know you must wonder about him sometimes."

"Some," I said, afraid that if I sounded too curious, she'd stop.

"He did have his good qualities." She began pulling cereal boxes off a shelf. "A great sense of humor, for one thing. And he was very good-looking in a cute big-puppy kind of way. You've seen those yearbook pictures, remember? A couple of years ago?"

I gave a guilty nod.

"He had a certain cockiness that a lot of girls like. He gave me presents, took me dancing." She laughed. "Said my name with this silly French accent." Mom cleared her throat. "Then I got pregnant. It took me a couple more months to admit it to myself, and another before I told him. Luckily, being pregnant took away my taste for alcohol and a lot of other things. . . ." She trailed off. She'd started on the spice rack, pulling out all the bottles and lining them up on the counter.

"What did he think?" I asked. "About a baby, about me?"

"By the time you were born, we weren't together anymore."

"Did he— Was he ever interested in me at all?"

"He gave me some money," Mom said. "And he made an effort to see you a couple of times. I think he cared, he just didn't know how to do anything with it. The caring, I mean. Oh, checks would turn up in the mail every now and then. Pretty nice checks. And I never hesitated to cash them. By the time I got the last one, I was working for Dr. Olson. Remember Dr. Olson?"

Of course I remembered her. She was the dentist Mom

worked for before I was old enough to go to school. Mom was her receptionist, and she used to take me to work sometimes. Other days Suzanne came over to baby-sit.

"The last time I saw Austin he was driving off in a BMW with some blonde."

No matter how hard I tried, I couldn't picture the tall guy in a BMW. For a second I considered telling her everything. But something—a shadow of uncertainty, a desire to keep him to myself, fear she'd prevent me from seeing him and wreck everything—kept me quiet.

"Okay, then," I said instead. "Thanks for telling me." I didn't know what else to say. Neither did Mom, apparently. She had pulled everything out of the kitchen cabinets.

Now we had to put it all back again.

•   •   •

That night I took the old Middlebrook yearbook out from under my mattress, where I'd hidden it the day I got grounded. I opened to Austin Trantor's class picture and tried to imagine what was going on behind the Ray•Bans. Did he wear them because he was stoned, or just cocky? I found Mom's picture in the sophomore section. Renee Pearce. She looked too young to be anybody's mother. Her hair was longer then and carefully curled, and she wore these big silver earrings and a black shirt that slipped off one shoulder. Austin and Renee, Renee and Austin. I could imagine them together on some smoky dance floor with a disco ball turning overhead, or sitting at a little table drinking from tall odd-shaped glasses, nuzzling each other. What did they talk about? Music, sports, nurdles?

What did they fight about? And how was it when she told him she was pregnant? Did he yell at her? Did he give her a kiss? Did he just walk away?

●　　●　　●

"Suzanne's here!" Vivian shouted from the top of the basement stairs the next morning. I'd just gotten out of the shower. "She wants her shoes."

It had been over a month since the Spring Fling fiasco, and even though Mom had made a big deal about me getting Suzanne's shoes back from Annie's, she'd forgotten about them once they were boxed up and ready to go.

"Sorry to take so long." I handed Suzanne the box with the silver ankle-straps inside.

"Don't worry about it. I don't think I've worn them more than twice since I bought them. I was glad you could use them," she said, then added, "even though you didn't. Renee here?"

"She's at work."

"Good." Suzanne pulled a white paper bag out of her canvas tote. "Chocolate-covered donuts were two for one at Safeway. I bought four. Got a cup of joe around here?"

Suzanne was dressed for work. Her radio mike crackled on her shoulder. As I poured two cups of coffee, I couldn't help thinking of all those donut-eating cops on TV. Except Suzanne was slim and pretty and had a good colorist.

"So who's this guy you're going out with tonight?" I asked.

"His name's Dennis. He's a Realtor." She licked chocolate off her thumb.

"How'd you meet him?" I asked. "Mom set you up?"

"We ran into him at lunch the other day, then he just called."

"Where are you going?" I asked. "Somewhere fancy, I guess, considering the shoes."

"Jazz cruise on Lake Coeur d'Alene. Dancing, dinner."

"So, do you like him?"

"Yeah. I do. How much, I don't know yet." Suzanne dates a lot, but she hasn't had a steady boyfriend in a while. The last one, a guy named Ernie, turned out to be gay. She was very supportive when he came out, and they're still good friends, but it made her kind of cautious.

"You knew my dad, right?" I asked before I had time to think about what I was saying. I guess the fact that my head was so full of him made it easy for him to spill right out. "My real dad. Austin Trantor."

"I met him twice. Once when I visited Renee at Middlebrook. I was in high school then. And once when he came to see you."

"What was he like?"

"Boy, that was a long time ago," she said. "Very cute, very funny, a real charmer. We threw a Frisbee out in the quad. It was just getting dark, and the air felt warm and peaceful, and your mom kept laughing and laughing. I remember that. I could certainly see why Renee was so taken with him. I was half in love with him myself," she said, shaking her head.

"And the second time?"

"That time Renee asked me to be there. He didn't stay very long."

"Why'd she ask you to be there?"

Suzanne screwed her mouth to one side and thought about it for a minute. "I think she needed moral support. It was hard for her to see him again." I wanted her to say something more, but she stood up abruptly. "Just look at the time. I've got to go to work, Stringbean. You still on probation?"

"Incarcerated's more like it."

"We'll call it being under house arrest." She laughed. "Don't worry, you'll be free soon."

If I don't bust out of here, I thought, and waved as she backed out of the driveway.

Sitting at the kitchen table finishing up the donuts, I wondered why it had been so hard for Mom to see Austin that time. She couldn't have still been in love with him. It had been so long, and she had Tony by then. Or could she? Maybe she needed Suzanne to help her stay strong, stay true to Tony when the real love of her life came back into her life. I had the feeling I wasn't getting the whole picture about their relationship. There was something about Austin Trantor she and Suzanne didn't want me to know.

chapter 8

nicholas finally called that night. Tony handed me the phone and tapped his watch to remind me I was still grounded. I took the cordless phone downstairs with me. Mine, an ancient pink princess phone that had once been Mom's, had been confiscated as part of my grounding.

"Hey, how are things going?" he asked.

"Terrible," I said. Although I'd been practicing all kinds of sharp things to say when he called, I was too glad to hear his voice to really get mad at him for waiting so long. "I'm totally grounded and I can only talk for five minutes."

"Okay, then I'll be quick. First, sorry I haven't called, but I really didn't want to get your mother on the phone.

Basically I'm a wimp who's guilty of sheer cowardice, not abandonment. Next, I really miss you."

"I miss you too," I said. "I am so bored I can hardly stand it."

"Look, I got some information on the tall guy."

I dropped onto my bed. "Austin?"

"Whatever his name really is, he says it's John Arlen."

"He says? You actually talked to him?"

"At the Comix Shop. I was in there the other day and so was he. He just came up to me and started this conversation about Japanese superheroes. He knows a lot about comic books."

"Wow!" I couldn't believe this. "What else did you find out?"

"He's a freelance photographer. That's why he was at the Rescue Bowl. He's interested in capturing people in their everyday environments. He calls it immersion . . . something like that."

"He told you all this at the Comix Shop?"

"Some of it. I ran into him again at the Cuckoo's Nest. I was drinking a mocha before work and he asked to sit down with me and Mandy—you know how it gets crowded in there." The mention of Mandy gave me a little jolt, but I didn't have time to think about her now.

"Why did he change his name?"

"Well, he really could *be* John Arlen. He may not be Austin Trantor at all." Vivian was yelling from the top of the stairs that I had one minute left.

"I *know* he's my dad. I have no doubt in my mind," I whispered fiercely.

For a minute Nicholas was silent; then he said, "If you're sure, okay."

"Look, I've got to go," I said. "What if I call you later, like after midnight?"

"Isn't that kind of late? I don't think my parents would like it, and I know yours wouldn't."

"They won't know. Just turn off all the ringers on the phones at your house before you go to bed. I'll call at one o'clock sharp. Pick up as soon after one as you can." I'd done this before with Kim, lots of times. It works great if you synchronize your watches.

"Talk to you then," Nicholas said. "I miss you." Mom's footsteps were on the stairs.

"Me too," I said, and hung up.

•   •   •

Just before one o'clock I climbed the basement steps in the dark and punched in Nicholas's number on the cordless phone. I slid open the door to the deck and took the phone outside. It was a warm night, and the stars were winking brightly through the pine trees behind the house. A couple of dogs were barking to each other, and I wondered what they were talking about so late at night. I counted phone rings until I lost track. Where was Nicholas? What if he had forgotten? And then he picked up.

"This is Apple, Banana. Come in, Banana. Do you read me?"

"Shhh," I said, as if Mom and Tony might hear him. "It took you long enough."

"Just remind me to turn the ringers back on before we hang up, okay, Banana?"

"Okay," I laughed. Then I got serious. "So tell me all about Austin."

77

"John. We should call him John so when you meet him you won't accidentally call him by the wrong name." When I meet him. I felt a little tingle up my spine.

"Okay. *John*. What did you find out about John Arlen?"

"He's from Minnesota. He played basketball in college—I asked him that—but not at Middlebrook, at some other place. Or so he claims. I didn't really get the name of the school."

"Why not?"

"Hey, I didn't want to sound like I was interrogating the guy," Nicholas said. "Anyway, I know John Arlen is his legal name because I saw his driver's license when he pulled out his wallet to leave a tip at the Nest. He had his camera with him, so I asked about that. He said he shoots nature photos for calendars and does some advertising stuff. But candid portraits are his real interest. They are, and I quote, his 'passion.' He said he's had a bunch of gallery shows, mostly in the Southwest."

"What else?"

"Well, the big thing is he asked about you."

I swallowed. "About me? What did he say?"

"He said he'd seen me with you and Vivian. He wanted to know if you two were my sisters."

"What did you say?"

"I said you were my friend. My girlfriend. I hope that was okay."

"That was okay." My cheeks were warming up. Despite the general assumption at school that we were a couple, we'd never really talked about what we were before. But now he'd told someone I was his girlfriend, so I guess

I was. I couldn't help wondering if Mandy was sitting at the table when he said it.

"He wanted to know about Vivian, was she your sister or mine, and he asked about the parks around here. He likes to get pictures of kids playing. He showed me a couple of prints and they're really good."

"Do you think I'm crazy?" I blurted out. "I mean, do you think this is even possible? That my dad came back?"

"I don't know, Ginger. He sure looks like those pictures of your dad. I guess people change their names for a lot of different reasons."

I thought about what Mom had told me about my dad's past with drugs. If he'd been in legal trouble, if he'd gone to jail, he might have needed to start over once he got out. I could understand how a person might choose a new name to go with a new life.

"Maybe he's in the witness protection program," I ventured.

"Maybe he doesn't want you to know who he is," Nicholas said. "I mean, if he's your dad, maybe he wants to keep it a secret until he figures things out." That made sense too, but I didn't like the idea very much. Why couldn't he just tell me?

"When will your mom let you go out again?" Nicholas asked. "I've got no one to play dominoes with," he added, and I could almost hear him smiling.

"July tenth."

"John said he'd probably be around for another week at least. He's got an assignment on Hell's Canyon for *Outside Adventure* magazine. I don't know where he's staying, but he said he's at the Cuckoo's Nest most afternoons."

"Why isn't he out taking pictures in the afternoon?" I asked.

"Gosh, Ginger, I don't know." Nicholas sounded exasperated. "You need to talk to him yourself, don't you think? Maybe he'll tell you he's your dad, and if he's not . . ."

"He is," I said, feeling certain again.

"Do you think you could accidentally meet me at the Nest tomorrow, like at two or so?" Nicholas asked.

"Maybe. Mom's got to work, so I'll have Vivian with me. Maybe she'll let me take Vivi to a movie. We could walk down to the Diamond, see a matinee, then stop in for an ice cream at the Nest."

"I don't want you to end up grounded for the rest of the summer," Nicholas said. "I'll just be there. Maybe John will be there too."

Austin, I thought. Maybe Austin Trantor will be there too.

I sat out on the deck for a little while longer. The dogs had stopped barking, and the wind rustling the pine trees sounded like secrets whispered in the night. There was no way I could go to sleep. I was completely wired. Nicholas had called me his girlfriend. More important, I was about to meet my father. *If* I could take Vivian to the movie. *If* he showed up at the Cuckoo's Nest. *If* he didn't leave town. This sudden panic came over me, and for a second I wanted to call Nicholas back. But I knew that would be insane.

●   ●   ●

The next morning I got up earlier than usual. I hadn't gotten much sleep, but I wasn't at all tired. It was so early

Tony hadn't even left for work yet, and I could hear him and Mom in the kitchen talking quietly, clicking cups and saucers, rustling the newspaper. Vivi wasn't up yet, and the house seemed unusually peaceful.

"Good morning, Gin." Mom glanced up from the paper. "Sleep well?" I nodded and poured about half a cup of coffee and filled the rest of it with milk. Café con leche, Tony called it when he used to fix it for me when I was a little kid. I still drink coffee only if it's mostly milk.

"You remember that you need to keep Vivi today, don't you?" Mom asked.

I nodded again.

"Maybe you two could go to the park."

"How about a movie?" I suggested. "It's so hot at the park, and there's that new animated dinosaur movie at the Diamond." Mom screwed her mouth up like she does when she's making up her mind. "We could walk," I added.

"Let me think about it," she said, which usually means yes. I tried not to smile as I sprinkled blueberries over my cornflakes.

She decided to let us go and even gave me extra money for popcorn and sodas. Vivi loved the movie, but I could hardly sit through it, I was so anxious about meeting Austin. *If* he showed up. In the middle of the scene where T. rex was chasing a herd of velociraptors, it occurred to me that he might have already left town. I didn't want to get my hopes up. I wanted to be realistic. He might have gotten a new assignment, or he might have changed his mind about me. The movie finally ended with T. rex plummeting off a waterfall and the rest of the dinosaurs living happily and harmoniously ever after. So much for scientific accuracy, I thought, but we were finally free to go.

I had no trouble convincing Vivian to get ice cream even though she'd eaten a jumbo popcorn and slurped down a large Coke during the movie. While we walked the two blocks to the Cuckoo's Nest, she narrated the whole movie again, from the time the little dinosaur hatches from the egg to his dino wedding at the end. I wasn't paying attention to her. I was peering through the Nest's plateglass window. I could see Austin Trantor seated at a table, and Mandy behind the counter in a black halter top whipping up milk shakes, but no Nicholas. What was I supposed to do? All the other tables were taken. I couldn't just go up to Austin and say, "Hi, Nicholas has told me a lot about you." And I didn't want to sit at the counter being civil to Mandy either. I dawdled outside the door, trying to think of ways to stall Vivi until Nicholas arrived, but before I could stop her she pushed through the door, clanging the cowbells that hung on the doorknob, and headed up to the counter. Austin Trantor watched her. He picked up his camera and snapped a picture. A candid portrait.

"Hey, you made it." Nicholas came up behind me. "Bike tire flat," he said, panting. "Had to hoof it."

"He's here," I hissed.

"Then let's go in."

Austin nodded at Nicholas and touched his forehead with two fingers in a kind of salute when we came through the door. He was sitting at one of the larger tables, as if he were expecting someone to join him. His blond hair was loose around his shoulders, and he wore a denim shirt with the sleeves rolled up. The silver-and-turquoise bracelet I'd noticed at the Rescue Bowl circled his tanned wrist. As Nicholas introduced us, I watched his face for some sign that he knew me, but he just nodded again and said he was glad to meet me.

"I've been telling Ginger about your work," Nicholas said, looking at me encouragingly, like I needed to say something. I could think of nothing, absolutely nothing to say. "She's interested in photography," he added, which wasn't exactly true. I mean, I can appreciate good pictures, but I'm not exactly *interested* in the topic.

"Really? What kind of equipment do you have?" Austin asked. "Digital? Thirty-five millimeter?"

"I don't really *do* photography. I don't take pictures, really. I just like them." I was sounding completely lame, and I looked to Nicholas for help as Vivi came up to the table with a double scoop of bubble gum ice cream.

"You gotta go pay," she said, her lips covered in creamy pink.

"I'll be right back," I said. "Don't go away."

"I've got all the time in the world," Austin said, and smiled a lazy lopsided smile. Still, I felt like any minute he'd just vanish without me ever having a chance to talk to him. If only he'd tell me who he was. What was he waiting for, anyway? Was this a test to see if I remembered him? Should I just go ahead and call him Dad or something? I ordered a decaf latte, pulled a ten-dollar bill out of my back pocket, and put it on the counter in front of Mandy.

As I went back to the table, Austin nodded toward the counter. "Forgot your change," he said. His mouth turned up on one side in a half grin and his ice blue eyes crinkled at the corners.

"Oh, duh." I wheeled around and walked right into a chair, which clattered to the floor. Everyone in the Cuckoo's Nest turned to look at me. "Sorry," I said to no one in particular as I picked up the chair. I headed to the counter again, where Mandy counted out my change at an excruciating pace.

"Have a nice day." She smirked. I shoveled the change into my back pocket and tried to compose myself.

I don't know exactly what I'd been expecting, but the whole meeting was a little strange. Disappointing, even. Austin—or John Arlen—mostly talked about himself and all the cool places he'd been and the galleries where he'd shown his work. To tell the truth, I'd expected him to show a little more interest in me. Wasn't I the reason he was in Cottonwood Falls to begin with? But he seemed more interested in Nicholas and Vivian, who he photographed several times eating ice cream. After about twenty minutes he stood up and slung his camera bag over his shoulder.

"Work calls. Got to go," he said, and stuck out his hand. "Nice meeting you."

"You too," I said, shaking hands, hoping he wouldn't notice how sweaty my palms were.

We watched him cross the street and get into a light blue Mustang.

"What a cool car," I said as we walked down the sidewalk toward Curry Park. The weather was hot and dry and the asphalt streets seemed to shimmer in the distance.

"It's a sixty-eight, in mint condition," Nicholas said. "Drives like a dream."

I stopped. "What, have you ridden in it?"

"Not yet, but John promised me he'd give me a ride sometime soon. He even offered to let me take it for a spin on my own."

"You can't drive yet," I said, annoyed that they were so tight.

"I can drive, just not well." Nicholas grinned. He'd gotten his permit in May, but he hadn't had much practice yet. "We'll stay on the back roads." Vivian was skipping down the sidewalk ahead of us. I yelled at her crossly to stop at the corner.

"He didn't seem very glad to see me," I said. I knew I sounded whiny, but meeting Austin Trantor had been kind of a letdown.

"Maybe he's just being careful," Nicholas said. "Maybe he just wants to see if you'll remember him first."

"What am I supposed to say? 'John Arlen isn't your real name, is it? You had to change it for reasons you'd rather not talk about, but I know who you really are.' You think he'd appreciate that?" A thought flitted through my mind like a mosquito. Maybe he really is John Arlen and I'm making this whole thing up. I swatted at the idea, brushed it away. There was no question that he had come to Cottonwood Falls to find me, to get to know me. I just had to be patient and look for opportunities to help him along.

● ● ●

When I got back home, I pulled the yearbook out from under my mattress. I'd spent so much time looking at the picture of Austin Trantor doing a layup that the book just naturally fell open to that page. There he was, only a few years older than I was now, talented, athletic, good-looking, fun. Okay, so he had some problems. But lots of people make bad choices in college and turn out just fine. Actresses, presidents. And look at Mom. Unless you count me, she wasn't exactly living with the sins of her past. What would my life be like now if he had stayed around? I wondered. What would I be like?

●　　●　　●

That night at dinner I sat there just waiting for Vivi to say something to get me in trouble as she talked about the movie and going to get ice cream.

"We saw Nicholas there," she finally said, and I was oddly relieved to have it out.

Mom raised her eyebrows at me.

"We just ran into him," I said. "He works there, you know. He just sat with us for a couple of minutes."

Mom's lips tightened. "You're still grounded."

"I know."

"For another two weeks."

"I *know*."

"Okay, just don't forget it." Tony gave her a look that said That's enough, but she couldn't stop. "And don't forget the pool party Friday afternoon."

"I won't. I haven't," I said. But I had. In all the excitement of the past couple of days, I had completely forgotten about the last Sunbeam meeting until school started in the fall, a party at the Sherwood Apartments swimming pool. And of course I was in charge of activities.

chapter 9

even though the Sunbeams had melted down to about six semiregulars, Mom was expecting ten second graders, which is so typical. Have a party and the slackers come out of the woodwork. We were having it at the apartment complex where Suzanne lives. She had reserved the clubhouse for Friday afternoon. The pool was usually empty on weekdays, she said, and it would be a perfect place for the Sunbeams' party. Suzanne made a cake shaped like a sun and Mom bought all kinds of yummy, junky snacks, something she never does for her own family. There would be a piñata, also shaped like a sun, and I was in charge of that and other games. The Sunbeams all arrived in Popsiclebright swimsuits and yellow baseball caps, dragging huge beach towels across the parking lot. Once we'd herded them into the fenced pool area, Mom and Suzanne opened out two lounge chairs at the deep end of the pool in case anybody needed saving. Suzanne knows CPR and all that rescue stuff. While the Sunbeams tested the water, the adults talked and worked on their tans, which I reminded them was unhealthy.

"I'm using this," Mom said, slathering on some number-six-SPF deep-tanning oil. The straps of her black tankini were draped off her shoulders, and she smelled like a Mounds bar.

"Anything less than twenty-five is useless," I said.

"At our age it's too late to worry," Suzanne said with a laugh. She had on an electric green bikini, and she didn't look a thing like a security guard. "Could you bring me a seltzer from the cooler, Stringbean? Thanks a bunch."

"Me too," Mom piped up.

After I'd waited on the grown-ups, I lined the Sunbeams up in the shallow end and threw pennies for them to chase after. This lasted about three minutes. Then they were playing their own game of mermaids and monsters, which was fine with me. Contrary to what most adults believe, little kids don't like a whole lot of organization. I was glad to see the Sunbeams just being kids instead of having their consciousness raised and organizing to save the world. Today they were just a bunch of skinny little girls splashing and squealing and talking with snooty British accents, which is how they talk when they get into that imaginary world, don't ask me why.

I was sitting on the side of the pool, my legs cooling in

the blue water. I had my eyes on the mermaids, but my ears were on Mom and Suzanne. They were talking about the Fourth of July, which was about a week away.

"I don't know what to do about Ginger's being grounded," Mom said to Suzanne in a low voice. I could feel her looking at me to see if I was listening, which I was, but I didn't turn her way. I just splashed the water with my feet and looked obliviously across the pool to the parking lot. "I don't want her to miss the fireworks, but I can't just let this go."

"Why not?" Suzanne asked. "You weren't exactly Teen Angel yourself."

"I know, I know." I could imagine what Suzanne might be remembering about Mom and all the things she'd done when she was about my age. Having Nicholas in the basement was nothing compared to that. "I guess I'll let her go, then. Do you think I should let her invite Nicholas? I don't want Nick to think I'm the Wicked Witch of the West. It really wasn't his fault." This was basically true, but it made me mad that Mom would let Nicholas off the hook completely. It takes two to tango, or whatever she imagined we were doing down there.

"He's a great kid," Suzanne said. "Ginger could do a lot worse. And you know the whole thing was perfectly innocent."

"It's not that, it's the lying that really got to me."

"Well, what goes around comes around, as they say," Suzanne said. "But really, you have nothing to worry about. Ginger the teenager will be a breeze compared to Renee the teenager."

I kept my eyes on the Sunbeams as Mom and Suzanne got up off their lounge chairs and stretched.

"Ginger," Mom called, pushing her bathing suit straps into place, "Suzanne and I are going to fix the snacks. Get the girls out in a couple of minutes and have them dry off."

A few minutes after they went inside the clubhouse, Austin's Mustang pulled into the parking lot. I watched as he hopped out and touched two fingers to his forehead in that quirky salute of his. I glanced back at the clubhouse, then flashed a quick wave. He grinned and winked, then raised his camera and started snapping pictures. Vivi recognized him and ran over to the fence.

"Take my picture," she said, and struck an MTV-worthy pose. Austin snapped away while she pranced around like a miniature rock diva.

"Vivian," I called to her. "Come back over here now so you'll be ready for snacks." She gave Austin a quick wave, then ran over to me.

"I'm starving," she said, hopping from one foot to the other.

I glanced back and saw Austin snap one last picture before he got back in his car just as Suzanne opened the clubhouse door. Oh god—would she recognize him?

"Was that man taking pictures of the girls?" she asked, squinting over at the Mustang. "Is that what he was doing?"

"Who was taking pictures?" Mom asked from behind, a huge bowl of chips in her hands.

"That man," Suzanne said, nodding in the direction he'd gone. "He just drove off."

"Does he live here in the complex?" Mom asked, alarmed. "Did you recognize him?"

"It was just John," Vivian said.

Mom frowned. "John who?"

"John Arlen," I said, trying to sound nonchalant. "He's a friend of Nicholas, a photographer. He takes photos for calendars and magazines."

"What kind of calendars?" Mom asked.

"Nature calendars. And advertising work too," I added. "Pictures of houses for sale. Apartment complexes." It wasn't exactly a lie. For all I knew, he did do that sort of work. I could easily imagine it.

"Well, I don't like him taking pictures of the girls. There's probably a law against photographing people without permission," Mom said.

"He was more interested in getting shots of the clubhouse than of the girls," I said.

"Then why did he take off as soon as Suzanne showed up?"

"I'm sure there's nothing to worry about," Suzanne said lightly as she cut a big slice of yellow cake. "Who wants the first piece?"

What had happened was obvious. Austin hadn't wanted Mom to recognize him. He was avoiding her on purpose, and considering her reaction, he had probably done the smart thing.

The Sunbeams devoured all the cake, all the chips, all the sodas. They broke the piñata and filled up paper sacks with candy. After making them wait fifteen minutes to digest so they wouldn't drown from cramps, Mom let them back in the pool. Everybody knows that story about cramps has no medical basis. You'd think a woman who didn't believe in skin cancer wouldn't worry about someone drowning from cramps in the shallow end of a pool, but that's my mom for you. Completely inconsistent.

● ● ●

"How were the little mermaids?" Nicholas asked when he picked up the phone at one o'clock that night. We'd been phoning in secret ever since I told him how to do it. Only once had he forgotten to turn the ringers back on, but his parents never noticed.

"Wet, but easy." I thought about Austin Trantor standing at the fence with his camera, but something stopped me from mentioning it. He'd come to see me at Sherwood Apartments, not Nicholas. He'd given me the secret two-finger salute, as if to say *I'm here, I know who you are, just give me a little more time.*

"You seem quiet tonight," Nicholas said. "Everything okay?"

"I'm just sick of being grounded," I said. "And staying up until one every night makes me tired the next day."

"You don't have to call me."

"That's not what I mean. I like to call you."

Nicholas didn't say anything, and I couldn't tell if he was offended or just soaking up what I hoped sounded like a compliment. He was the only one who knew about Austin Trantor, the only one I could talk to, and I hoped he realized how much that meant to me.

"At least we've got the Fourth of July and fireworks coming up," I said. "You are coming, aren't you?" Mom had let me call him earlier that evening while she stood over me like a prison guard, listening to every word I said.

"Yeah. But I might be late."

"Why?"

"The Roscoes are having a barbecue. I have to stop by."

"Oh." I could just imagine Mandy Roscoe bouncing around the pool in a tiny black bikini, blond, perfectly tanned, hugging Nicholas every chance she got. "Don't feel like you *have* to come to the park. It's just a little family picnic," I said, trying to sound like it was no big deal.

"I *want* to come to the park. I want to be with you. The Fourth will be the first time in exactly fifteen days that I'll have a chance to see you without having to do it on the sly."

"You've been counting?"

"Haven't you?"

"Yeah." In fact, I'd been marking my calendar with big red Xs.

"I saw John at the Nest early this morning," Nicholas said. "I had first shift. He asked where you were."

"And?"

"I told him about the party at Sherwood. He had a shoot in Rye Plain. He was doing some old barns and antique farm equipment for a calendar. I think he was going to camp at Lake Roosevelt, maybe stay up there through the Fourth."

"He left this morning? And he's staying away through the Fourth?"

"That was the plan. Why?"

"Oh, no reason," I said. Rye Plain wasn't near the Sherwood Apartments. Did he make a special trip just to see me?

"I hope it won't rain for the Fourth," Nicholas said, distracting me from my thoughts. "Should I just meet you there?"

"Okay. I'll be down at the swings with Vivian."

"Good. I'll see you then. Sleep tight."

"You too," I said. "Bye."

I tiptoed back into my bedroom. The yearbook fell open to the picture of my dad making the winning layup that put Middlebrook College in the playoffs. That's what the caption said, anyhow, but how could I be sure? Maybe it was a picture of some other layup during some other game. Maybe it was just practice. The picture was kind of blurry, and my dad's mouth was open in a little O of concentration. His eyes were on the basket, and he hung in the air over the heads of all the other players. I flipped to the team picture and looked at his face again. If only that other player wasn't blocking him. I studied his ice blue eyes for a while, then turned to the class photo. It was impossible to see behind the dark glasses, but the nose, the chin, the mischievous mouth were clear. I still couldn't believe they let him wear sunglasses for his picture. But this was college. He was an adult. I guess there wasn't a lot they could do. From the three pictures I could piece him together, the pale blue eyes from the team shot, the jaw from the layup shot, and the nose and lopsided grin from the class picture. The blond hair in all three. I could picture him nodding at me from the pages, putting two fingers to his forehead in that cocky salute of his. John Arlen. Austin Trantor. Dad. "Where have you been all this time?" I whispered, tracing my finger over the picture of his face. "Why did you turn up now?" If you want to get in touch with me, you better hurry up, I thought. I'm running out of patience.

chapter 10

on july 3 I got two e-mails, one from Kim saying she'd fallen in love with a boy from Yakima, and one from Annie, who was getting a little out of control with Devon. Apparently they'd gotten matching tattoos on that part of the body where the sun never shines. Kim wanted me to write back ASAP with advice, but what was I supposed to tell her? I'd never been in her position before. Besides, her two-boyfriend problem seemed pretty trivial compared to what was going on in my life, which I couldn't tell her about. Not yet anyway. It was too complicated to get into over e-mail. *Don't even think about breaking up with Carter,* I typed instead. *Don't even mention this guy to him. Yakima Boy is a summer crush.*

Annie didn't want advice. She just wanted to show off. *Watch yourself, girl,* I typed back. *Stop sneaking out at night, and don't drink any more of those special cocktails he makes. And DON'T get any more tattoos. The boy is trouble.* I knew she'd laugh, flinging her long blond hair back from her face, but maybe she'd think about it too. If she's not careful, she'll end up just like my mom, with somebody like me to take care of one day.

"Both Annie and Kim have a bad case of ostrich eye," I told Nicholas on the phone that night.

He laughed. "How's that?"

"Summer crushes. Their eyes are bigger than their brains."

"Not like us," he said.

"Not a thing like us."

●　　●　　●

The Fourth of July dawned with pouring rain. Even after the rain stopped, the clouds hung around into the afternoon, and it was cool enough for jeans and a sweatshirt.

"You think they'll cancel?" Tony asked almost hopefully.

"It's going to be beautiful," Mom said. "Just wait." And she was right. By three o'clock the sky was perfectly clear, the air was warm, and Mom and Suzanne were headed down to the park with Vivian. They had packed up cherries, trail mix, and chocolate chip cookies.

"I thought you weren't supposed to take alcohol to the park," I said as I watched Mom pour a bottle of chardonnay into a large thermos.

"Suzanne and I are responsible adults. A couple glasses of wine won't turn us into raving lunatics. Besides, everyone does it. And no one will know." If I'd used those arguments, I'd have gotten a lecture. Or two—one on not following the crowd and one on not trying to get away with things just because you can.

"Nicholas is meeting me around five-thirty near the playground," I said. "I'll be down in a little bit."

"Your seats are reserved, Stringbean." Suzanne gave me one of her chocolate chip cookies as she walked out the door. That cheered me up. Nobody bakes cookies like Suzanne.

Tony stood at the sink chopping pimentos for his special hot pimento-cheese sandwiches. He'd put some Latin jazz on the CD player and was doing a salsa step while he chopped in time with the music.

"You can buy those already diced, you know," I told him.

"Yeah, but they're not as good."

"What's the difference?"

"They put mostly the end pieces in the jars of diced pimentos. These are plumper."

I wondered how Tony would know something like that. Maybe he was just making it up, but it was probably true. Tony knows all kinds of trivial food facts, like what fruit has the most antioxidants and where the best macadamia nuts come from. Plus he's probably the most honest person I know. He'd never make anything up, not even about diced pimentos.

"You want to get the cheddar cheese out of the fridge for me?" I handed him a large block of sharp cheddar. "So are you and Nicholas going steady?"

97

I made a face. "People don't go steady anymore, Tony."

"So what do you do, then? Date? Go together? Hook up?"

"We're just good friends," I said.

"Oh, I see. I've heard that one before." Now he was grating cheese in time with the music, his hips moving to a rumba beat.

"Okay, I like him better than any other guy I know. He's really different. I mean, I can talk to him, tell him stuff, and he listens. Guys aren't always good at that, you know." Tony nodded. "Not that I've had a lot of experience with guys," I added. "It's like I can tell him stuff I might not even tell Annie or Kim. Plus he makes me laugh."

"Good kisser?" Tony asked.

"Tony!"

"Just kidding. I really wouldn't want to know. He seems like a good guy. And I know good guys are not all that easy to find. I mean, not every man can be a Tony Rosa."

I laughed and swatted him with a dish towel. He forked up a dollop of his pimento cheese. "Perfecto," he said, holding out the fork for me. It was great, hot and smoky, a little like Mr. Blackstone's thom yum goong.

"I just wish Mom would trust me more," I said. "I mean, Nicholas and I don't do anything, not like what she thinks we do."

"Your mom just wants you to be careful. Seeing you at this age, on the verge of some big decisions about your life, it makes her nervous."

"What's she scared of? That I'll be like she was at fifteen?" After I said it, I was afraid I'd gone too far. But Tony just smiled and shook his head.

"That's some of it. Try to see it from her point of view."

"I know. I do try. But it doesn't mean I'm just like her. I'm only half her," I added.

Tony nodded but didn't say anything. Maybe he was thinking that the other half wasn't even worth mentioning. But I had a right to decide that for myself.

●　　　●　　　●

When I got to Curry Park, Mom and Suzanne were set up near the gazebo where the band would play. They were engrossed in some serious gossip while Vivi lay stretched out on her stomach, dressing Ballerina Star Barbie in the new red-white-and-blue evening gown Suzanne had brought her. Vivi's hair was tied up in high curly pigtails with red, white, and blue ribbons. Mom waved a container of trail mix at me, her way of acknowledging that I had arrived. Vivian popped to her feet immediately.

"Yay! Swings!" she said. "I was getting really bored."

Suzanne unfolded another lawn chair. "Hang on, Vivi, let Ginger grab a soda and sit with us a minute." She said it like she really meant it, and she probably did. Suzanne likes to have me and Vivian around, and it's not just because she's our aunt. She likes our company. Mom, on the other hand, didn't say anything, so I figured I'd just be interrupting if I stayed.

"That's okay," I said. "I'll go ahead and take Vivi to the playground." Vivian turned a perfect cartwheel and ran ahead of me toward the swings and slides.

"Don't let her out of your sight!" Mom called out.

I didn't even bother to answer. I've been baby-sitting Vivi since I was about ten years old. I knew what to do at least as well as Mom did.

The playground was on the far side of the duck pond, about a quarter mile beyond the gazebo where Mom and Suzanne were yakking and drinking their illegal wine. The park maintenance crew had roped off a large area nearby, where they were putting the finishing touches on the fireworks. There were a ton of kids down there watching the men work, and even more on the play equipment, and lots of moms sitting around chatting. All the benches were taken, so I sat in a shady patch of grass out of the traffic and waited for Nicholas to show up. The basketball court was packed with dads trying to teach their little kids to shoot; the soccer field crawled with Frisbee tossers and baseball throwers. Every now and then I'd lose sight of Vivi in the sea of kids, but then she'd resurface. She always attracts a crowd, even though she's the bossiest little girl I know. They flitted from swings to slide to monkey bars like a flock of bright birds.

I'd kind of zoned out, sitting there in the shade, a warm breeze lifting my hair off my forehead, when I felt Nicholas squeeze my shoulder from behind. I put my hand on his, smiled, and turned around. And realized it wasn't Nicholas at all. It was Austin Trantor. I jerked my hand away as a wave of embarrassment broke over me.

"I thought . . ." I trailed off, fumbling for words.

"You thought I was Nicholas. Sorry to disappoint you." He laughed lightly. His pale blue eyes pierced me like icicles and I had to look away. "I didn't mean to startle you. I shouldn't have come up behind you like that. Forgive me?"

"No big deal, really. My mistake," I said, trying to sound casual when I was really shaking inside from being so close to him and alone. He had a bandana tied loosely around his neck, and the silver bracelet shone against his tanned wrist. Up close I could see the fine gold hairs on his arm, the copper freckles sprayed across his nose, the laugh lines that creased the corners of his eyes. I could imagine him at twenty-one, the way he looked when Mom met him. I could imagine him at my age, tall and skinny and maybe a little goofy, like Nicholas is sometimes.

"Quite a crowd," he said, sitting down next to me. His camera hung around his neck.

"Here to get some shots?" It was a lame question, but I had to say something. I didn't want him to think I was a total imbecile.

"I like crowds," he said.

"Crowds of kids especially," I said, trying again, thinking of the pool party.

"Children are wonderful subjects," he said, looking through his camera lens at the playground. "They're so uninhibited. They don't get hung up about being in front of the camera." He clicked the shutter. "They don't care what they do, really."

"Like Vivian at the pool the other day," I offered.

"Like Vivian," he said, still scanning the playground through his lens. "The camera loves her, and the camera is very particular."

What was I supposed to say to that? He'd shown no interest whatsoever in taking my picture, but he couldn't keep his camera off Vivi.

"I thought you were going to Rye Plain to shoot some

old tractors and stuff," I blurted out, surprised at the accusation in my voice.

He brought the camera down from his face but kept his gaze focused on the playground. "The weather wasn't right. Not enough light, the right kind of light. I had to postpone the shoot."

"That's too bad," I said.

"Not really."

I wished Nicholas would show up, because this conversation was grinding to a painful halt. I could think of nothing to talk about, or more accurately, the one thing I couldn't talk about was the only thing that came to mind.

"So where are you from?" I asked.

"I'm not from anywhere, really," he said. "I've been around."

"You have to be from somewhere," I prodded. "Originally, I mean."

"East Coast. Rhode Island," he said. "Providence."

I knew he wasn't telling the truth, not only because he was really from Tacoma and went to Middlebrook College, not only because he'd told Nicholas he was born in Minnesota—another lie—but because of the way he said it, taking a stab at some region of the country first, then coming up with the state and city. I was starting to feel pissed off about the whole thing. He was my *father*, for crying out loud, and he wasn't being at all honest with me. He wasn't being fair or even very considerate. Here we were, pretty much alone. This would be the perfect time to let me know who he really was. I wouldn't tell anybody, if he wanted to keep it between the two of us. I could be trusted.

Then it occurred to me that maybe he had searched me out here, alone, to give *me* the opportunity to let him know *I* knew who he was. Sure, it seemed complicated, but the whole situation was complicated. Maybe I just needed to make the first move. I took a deep breath.

"I don't think you are from Rhode Island," I said, trying to keep my voice light, like we were just kidding around.

"Don't you, now?" He glanced at me, a split second slash of ice blue. His mouth turned down a little.

"No. I think you're from somewhere a lot closer."

He smiled. "What makes you think so?"

"I have my reasons. And I don't think John Arlen is your real name."

He shifted in the grass. It was hard to tell what he was thinking as he looked at me carefully.

"Who am I, then?"

"You're Austin Trantor."

"And who is Austin Trantor?" he asked in the simple voice he might use with a small child.

"My father," I whispered, then said a little louder, "You're my father."

For a minute I thought he might deny it. Then his face softened and he turned away from me, closing his eyes. Vivi was standing at the top of the slide and I thought, Okay, now she'll fall and I'll have to run see about her. Right here at the most important moment in my life she'll break her neck and Austin will go away and I'll never see him again. But she didn't. She went down the slide, and my dad opened his eyes and put a gentle hand on my arm.

"You are a clever girl, Ginger." He gave my arm a

squeeze. "How did you figure it out?" I was so relieved I started laughing and felt my eyes tear up at the same time. He started laughing too. He'd been waiting for this moment, just like I had. He was waiting to be recognized.

"I've got pictures. Mom told me all about you."

"She did?"

"Well, not *all* about you, but a lot."

"What did she say?" His mouth curled into the same mischievous smile of the twenty-one-year-old in the yearbook.

"Well," I said, trying to choose my words wisely, "she told me how you met at Middlebrook and how you were this great basketball player. You played center."

"That was a long time ago." He took my hand in his. It felt strange, but I couldn't pull away. He was my dad, after all.

"And she told me how you had lots of friends and were a great dancer and had a great sense of humor." I wiped my eyes. "And how you liked to pronounce her name the French way."

He kept nodding, a sad smile playing around his lips. "Your mother and I were very close at one time. Did she tell you how we broke up?"

"Not really, no details."

"Maybe I'll tell you that story one day." He eyelids fluttered, as if to blink away tears. "It was a hard thing, a very difficult thing, to leave you. Your mother, does she know I'm in town?"

"Oh no, I don't think so. She didn't see you at the pool the other day. You left just in time. Suzanne saw you, but she didn't recognize you."

"Ah, Suzanne, Suzanne," he said, probably remembering the time they threw the Frisbee in the twilight at Middlebrook fifteen years ago.

"You probably don't remember her very well. I mean, she was still in high school when you met Mom."

"Suzanne? No, but your mom talked about her quite a bit." He dropped my hand gently. "And Vivian, where does Vivian come in?"

"It was just Mom and me after you left. Then she met Tony and they got married. Vivian was born when I was eight." I looked up at him. "I'm fifteen now," I added.

"Yes, I know. You've grown into a lovely young lady, Ginger." He smiled and pushed my hair away from my cheek. "Is your mother here? With Tony?"

"Tony's coming later. Mom's up near the gazebo with Suzanne saving me a spot. I'm just baby-sitting Vivian."

"Ah, the beleaguered older sister." He smiled. "You're very close to her, aren't you?"

"To Vivi? Yeah, I guess. I take care of her a lot, anyhow."

"Family. It's such a gift. And we have a way of taking it for granted, don't we?" He shook his head slowly and watched the children playing.

"I don't guess you want to see Mom?" I said. "I could go get her if you do."

He hesitated, then shook his head. "No, not just yet."

I nodded. Honestly, I was relieved not to have to bring her into it. Just getting used to the idea that he was my dad was overwhelming enough.

"But you did hope to see me here?" I asked, feeling shy.

"You're why I agreed to take the assignment here. Ever since I got to Cottonwood Falls, I've been waiting for the right time." He smiled at me, but he kept glancing around too, like he was afraid Mom might walk up any minute. He just wasn't ready to deal with her yet, and I could understand that. "I've thought of you endlessly over the years, Ginger. When can I see you again?"

"Tomorrow? How about at the Cuckoo's Nest?" I could figure out some excuse to leave the house. Vivian would have to come along, but that was only a small inconvenience.

He shook his head. "Won't work. I'll be in Rye Plain making up the shoot I had to postpone. Is there another time?"

"Mom and Tony will be gone Monday morning," I told him. "But maybe you don't want to come to our house."

He shrugged. "No, that would work. I could drop by, if you think it's all right."

I gave him my address, which he wrote down in a small black notebook. Then he stood up and brushed off his jeans.

"You're leaving?" I asked, disappointed.

"I've got dinner plans. But I'll see you Monday. About ten o'clock?" He took my hand again and squeezed it.

"See you then," I said, then whispered, "Dad."

•　　•　　•

About five minutes after Dad left, Nicholas rode up on his bike. It seemed like the whole world had changed in the past half hour. I couldn't wait to tell him everything, but Vivi ran up as soon as she saw him, and I had to wait.

"Swing me around, Nicholas, swing me around!" she shouted, hanging on to his leg. He swung her until she was dizzy and weaving and laughing; then he plopped down on the grass beside me.

"I saw my dad. Austin," I said in a low voice. "He had a lot to say."

"Like what?"

I nodded toward Vivian, who had regained her balance and was rushing toward us again.

"Go find a swing, Viv," Nicholas shouted. "I'll be there in a minute and I'll give you a big push, okay?" She took off for the swings, her curly black pigtails bouncing. "So what's up? I thought he was still in Rye Plain."

I told Nicholas everything. It was easy to repeat all we'd said, impossible to express the feelings underneath the words.

He let out a low whistle. "So it's true? He is your dad?"

"Of course it's true," I said. "Did you ever really doubt it?"

"Well, didn't you?"

"Never!" It hurt that Nicholas questioned my intuition. It hurt that he might think I was chasing some crazy idea, some make-believe dream about my father. And it hurt that he hadn't told me about his doubts. Still, it *was* pretty incredible that my father would locate me after all those years, that he would trust me to recognize him, that he would trust me not to betray him to Mom or anyone until he was ready. Considering how the whole situation was just short of miraculous, I could kind of understand Nicholas's uncertainty.

Nicholas squeezed my arm. "Don't be mad. This is really cool." He rummaged around in his backpack and pulled out a large gold envelope.

"What is it?"

"It's a little something from me. And John. I mean Austin."

From the envelope I pulled out a glossy black-and-white photograph of Nicholas. It was a great shot. Nicholas's arms were crossed on the roof of the Mustang, his chin resting on his arms. His black hair was lifted just a little by the wind; his eyes sparkled. In the background stood an old barn and a couple of cottonwood trees.

"Wow, that is fantastic. He's really good," I said, flooding with pride. Nicholas's cheeks turned pink. "Hey, you're blushing," I teased him.

"I'm not used to being a model. It's not bad, though, is it? He said to give it to my girlfriend."

• • •

Everything was perfect that night: Tony's hot pimento-cheese sandwiches and crispy fried chicken. The sweet Bing cherries and Suzanne's chocolate chip cookies. The band music that sent all the little kids marching around lawn chairs and blankets. The cool breeze that lifted as the sun went down, and the fireworks like hundreds of giant stars flowering overhead. Fireworks blooming red, purple, orange, and green, with the bitter smell of smoke and sharp explosions that made our hearts race. Nicholas and I lay on our backs holding hands, pointing at the magnificent colors.

"You know what makes that one green?" Nicholas asked, his lips close to my ear. "Barium. The silver ones, those come from magnesium and aluminum."

"What about that one?" I asked as a red rocket burst like a giant chrysanthemum overhead.

"That's strontium. And that," he said, pointing to a llow burst, "that's sodium."

Barium, strontium, aluminum, sodium. The words caressed my ear like poetry spoken in some foreign language. I turned my head toward him. "What makes you so smart?"

"I don't know." He turned his head toward me so our noses touched. "What makes you so sweet? And pretty? And fun to be around?"

"I don't know."

"I don't know either," he whispered, and gave me a long secret kiss in the dark.

chapter 11

that whole weekend I kept spacing out. I just couldn't concentrate on anything but Monday morning. Finally Mom yelled at me for not paying attention to her and threatened to ground me for longer if I didn't shape up. That got me focused, and I spent Saturday afternoon and most of Sunday cleaning up my room and the bathrooms, mowing the lawn, and doing laundry just to make her happy. I didn't mind, really. I just kept thinking about being with my dad. I had about a million things to ask him. What was his childhood like? What were my grand-arents like? When did he decide to look for me?

made a list of all the things I needed to know: his

favorite color, his favorite food, the kind of music he listened to. I looked at the pictures dozens of times and tried
to remember everything Mom had told me, especially the
good stuff. Though you couldn't ignore the bad stuff.
Using and selling drugs, there was no way to romanticize
that. Why had he been away so long? Had he been in jail?
Rehab? I knew I'd heard only one side of the story. Mom's.
But he could fill in the rest and help me understand the
real reason why he left, why he'd waited so long to get
back in touch. Now that he'd found me, I could forgive
anything.

●　　●　　●

Tony and Mom left for work early Monday morning.
Mom had some houses to show and wouldn't be back until
midafternoon; Tony would be home at the usual time,
right before dinner. I had hoped Vivi would be invited to
play over at someone's house, but no one called. At ten
o'clock she was still in her pajamas, driving her Barbie car
up and down the stairs. When the doorbell rang, I nearly
jumped out of my skin, even though I'd been checking the
clock every five minutes for the past half hour. I opened
the door nervously.

And there he was. He looked almost as excited as
I was.

"Ginger, honey, you look great," my dad said, taking
both my hands. I was pleased he noticed. I'd curled my
hair and put on a little makeup once Mom left. I had on
my favorite blue sleeveless top and white shorts. His
hands holding mine felt warm and sure.

"Come on in," I said, then added, "Mom and Tony left a while ago." I didn't want him to feel nervous about being there.

"Hey!" Vivi shouted from the top of the stairs, and let her pink Barbie convertible bump down the steps and crash at the bottom, where Barbie and Ken were thrown from the car. "Want to take my picture?"

"Not today, short stuff. But those pj's are awfully cute. Who's that on the front of your shirt?"

Vivian stuck her chest out. "Belle, from *Beauty and the Beast*." My dad grinned and winked at her.

I'd set the dining room table with my favorite ivy-patterned tablecloth and the good white cups and saucers rimmed in silver. As soon as Mom had left I'd made a batch of muffins and picked a bunch of daisies for the table.

"Would you like some coffee?" I asked, hoping I didn't sound too formal.

"Want to see my room?" Vivian asked.

"Maybe in a little bit," my dad answered, and tousled her hair.

"Muffin?" I asked, wishing Vivian would disappear for an hour, just one hour. There were things Dad and I needed to discuss.

"Well, this is a real treat," he said, finally turning his attention to the table. "Did you make these?"

"I did. They're from a mix, but they're really good," I said. "Sugar or milk in your coffee? We don't have cream."

"Just black." Instead of sitting down, my dad ambled around the living room, looking at the photographs that decorated our mantel and walls: baby pictures of me and

Vivian, school portraits, a large wedding picture of Mom and Tony under an arbor of white flowers. He looked at that one for a long time and said Mom was just as pretty as ever. None of the pictures were very professional-looking, and I was embarrassed for him to see them, considering the fabulous work he produced.

"And what does Tony do?" he asked as we sat down at the table and Vivian ran off to her room. I told him about Mom's job, about school and basketball and Kim and Annie, about Nicholas and being grounded. It was like I couldn't tell him everything fast enough. He nodded as he took in the details of the room, and I wished I lived in Nicholas's house with its carpets and piano and really good photographs.

"Tell me about you and Mom," I said, sitting down next to him. "Why didn't things work out? Unless you don't want to talk about it . . ."

"Oh, that was so long ago." He stirred his coffee absently. "And I'm sure she's told you much of the story."

"Well, to be honest, she hasn't told me a lot. I know you met at college and dated and then I came along. That's about it."

"And then I left, abandoning you. Is that what she says?"

"Well, yeah. I guess that's how she sees it."

He shook his head. "That is so typical. It was your mother who took you from me. *I* wanted to marry her. *I* wanted us to be a family." He turned his silver bracelet around on his wrist, traced the pattern with his finger, and was quiet for a few minutes. "She has her reasons for making it sound like I was the bad guy. And I know things might not have worked out if we'd stayed together, but I swear to you, I loved you the first time I set eyes on you. I still love you."

It *was* so typical of my mom, only seeing things her way. Refusing to compromise. A bubble of anger rose up inside me. What would things have been like if she'd looked outside herself just once?

We stood up at the same time and hugged. My dad rubbed his hands up and down my back and held me to him tightly. When Vivian came in to get a muffin, he let go of me and picked her up. She hugged him hard around the neck.

"I just want you," he said, stroking Vivian's hair, his voice unsteady. "I want you with me, Ginger." Gently he brushed my hair back from my face. He put Vivian down and wiped his eyes with the back of his hand. "I really can't stay any longer." I understood how hard this was for him. It was hard for me too.

"When will I see you again?" I asked, trying not to sound desperate.

"We'll figure it out, honey. I can't make any promises right now. I don't want to make promises I can't keep."

"Where are you staying? Can I come there?"

"I've been staying at a friend's house, out in the country. It would be impossible for you to get out there without a car," he said. "I'll be in touch." He hugged me again. "Don't worry. We'll work something out. This is just between us. For now. Is that okay?"

I nodded.

"Can you keep a secret, pretty Vivian?"

She nodded too, and my dad stroked her black curls.

As he drove away, I thought about all the things I hadn't had a chance to ask him, so many facts of his life and mine I still didn't know. Most importantly, when would I see him again?

• • •

Despite Vivian's promise, you can never trust a seven-year-old with a secret.

"Vivian told me this photographer fellow—the one who was hanging around the Sherwood pool—was here today," Mom said later that afternoon. "What is this all about, Ginger?"

"What photographer?" I asked, stalling. Aside from the fact that I didn't want her to know about Austin Trantor, I only had two more days of being grounded and I didn't want to blow it.

She frowned. "How many do you know?"

"Oh, Au— Arlen. John Arlen. Yeah, he was in the neighborhood and he dropped off a CD I'm borrowing from Nicholas."

"Vivian says you let him in the house."

"I, um, yeah. I had to go down to the basement to get a CD for him to take back to Nicholas. We traded." Mom looked appalled. "What was I supposed to do?" I said. "Leave him on the doorstep?"

"Ginger, what were you thinking? Letting a total stranger into the house?"

"He's not a stranger. He's an old friend of Nicholas, of Nicholas's parents, really. A family friend. Remember I told you that earlier? I was just being polite. He didn't stay or anything," I ventured, hoping Vivian hadn't gone into great detail.

"You need to be more careful," Mom said. "You can't trust just anyone."

"I know," I said, exasperated. "I would never let a total stranger in the house."

"I know you wouldn't do anything dangerous on purpose," she said, shaking her head. "But often it's not the total strangers you have to worry about. It's the people you think you know."

"Like Austin Trantor," I couldn't help saying. She looked surprised to hear his name.

"Like Austin Trantor." She sighed. "A man I thought I knew well."

I didn't say anything else. I honestly felt bad about lying to Mom, especially when it was such a big lie. But what else could I do? My dad wasn't a stranger, not anymore.

For Mom, Austin was the man who left us. For me, Austin Trantor was a man who hadn't been given a chance, a man who had come a long way just to find the daughter he loved. A man who would never hurt anyone. A man who'd given me life.

And somehow I'd need to make her see that.

chapter 12

the next morning I took Vivian down to Curry Park. I had a hunch that Dad might show up there, and I was right.

"Hello, ladies," he said as he jogged up to the swings and gave Vivi a little push. "Smile!" He snapped her picture, then turned to me. "Say cheese!" I grinned as he pressed the button. He put his camera back into his black bag and began pushing Vivian. I sat in the swing next to her, facing him, and swayed back and forth while we talked. And we talked about everything. About his family, about growing up in Tacoma. He talked about his work and his love for nature and children. After a while Vivian got tired of swinging and ran to the big slide. Dad and I sat down on the grass. It had just been mowed and smelled like summer.

"Have you ever been married?" I asked, feeling a little shy.

"Once, for a short while. I met a pretty lady with a little girl about Vivian's age. It didn't work out, though."

"Why not?"

"Oh, I don't know. We were both hardheaded, I guess. Couldn't see many things eye to eye."

"Do you still see the girl? Your stepdaughter?"

"No. Her mother decided she didn't want me to. There wasn't much I could do about that, seeing as she wasn't mine. I always wanted a family," he said. "Losing you and your mother was real rough for me. It took a long time before I could trust folks again."

"I wish things could have been different," I said.

"So do I, sweetheart." He stared off across the playground. "I didn't even know where to find you for quite a while there."

"She didn't tell me that."

"No. I don't expect she would. She's got her version of things, just like I've got mine. And I guess she had her reasons."

"What if we talk to her?" I suggested. "Maybe we could work things out so I could be with you more. I don't mean live with you or anything, but just visit you sometimes." I had a quick vision of riding in the blue Mustang through a desert landscape of red mesas, flowering cacti, and sagebrush.

"We'll talk to her when the time is right," he said. "Don't worry. It'll happen."

Before he left, my dad said he'd be in touch. I wanted to know how.

He grinned at me. "Don't you know I'll always be able to find you?"

"We'll be here," I called after him as he walked off. He touched two fingers to his forehead and saluted but didn't look back.

•   •   •

And so the next day was like the one before, a long talk sitting on the cool grass in the shade of a giant pine tree, Vivian swinging and singing to herself, a breeze whispering through the treetops. Dad had brought a small cooler of sodas, a bag of chips, and some apples and cheese. "Not a full-blown picnic," he apologized, "just a little something for grazing."

He showed me some of his latest prints: a tractor with the sun setting behind it, a funny close-up of a cow. He had about a dozen prints of this old barn, really nice shots taken at strange angles. I liked those the best.

Talking to him was more like talking to a big brother than to a parent. I could tell him anything: how I felt about Nicholas, how Mom and I had our problems. He'd had similar experiences when he was young. His father kept a tight rein and insisted that he get involved in Boy Scouts and the debate team and other things he had no interest in.

"My father expected me to become a lawyer like himself, but I knew that wasn't me," he said. "I wasn't interested in controlling people or making them believe things. I just wanted to figure out who I was and be that person. 'Live and let live' has always been my motto. It takes all kinds to make a world, and people should get in touch with who they really are before they start trying to change other people's opinions and habits."

"Yeah, I know what you mean," I said, thinking of Mom trying to mold the Sunbeams into her definition of model citizens. "It's just hard sometimes to figure out what to get in touch with."

He laughed. "Oh, you'll figure it out."

"How do you know?"

"You're a lot like me, I think. You just need to remember there's a great big world out there, Ginger." He balanced an apple on the tips of his fingers. "Think of the world as your apple. You've got to take a big bite of it one day. It might be sweet, it might be bitter, but one thing for sure is you've got to try it. You have to look farther than your own backyard, know what I mean?"

"That's kind of hard to do when they won't let you out of the fence," I said.

He cut the apple into slices with a fancy hunting knife. The handle was inlaid with onyx and turquoise, the blade sharp and shiny. With the tip of the blade he speared a slice of apple and offered it to me.

"Your parents see things from only one perspective," he said. "You'll find your way soon enough." Taking a red bandana from his back pocket, he wiped the blade of the knife clean. "See this bowie knife? This was given to me by a Navajo shaman the night he died. His name was Truman Coyote. He told me any fruit cut with this knife would make the one who ate the fruit fruitful himself."

"Fruitful how?" I asked, biting into the cool, sweet apple.

"Fruitful in mind and body. Creative and healthy. Full of the life force."

"Wow, do you think that's true?"

"Energy moves through the universe in mysterious ways. The life force brings opportunity to those who wait." He smiled and cut himself a slice of apple. "Maybe you can find out for yourself, now that you've eaten the fruit cut by the shaman's knife."

•　　•　　•

"That is so cool," Nicholas said that night when I told him about the shaman's knife. We were shooting baskets in his driveway under a big yellow floodlight. My weeks of being grounded were finally over, and it felt great to be free.

"Do you think the knife could really have special powers?" I asked.

"Sure. Those shamans are for real. You can find those guys all over the world—Africa, South America, among native tribes here. It's more than just some religion. They really do have powers we can't understand."

"You know, if my dad had stayed around after I was born, if he'd married Mom, or even if he hadn't, I would have had a very different life."

"Maybe you ought to let your mom know he's here," Nicholas said.

I shook my head. "Like he says, when the time is right, we'll let her know." I passed him the ball. "Just think about it. I could be living in an adobe house in the desert. Or I might have traveled around the whole country— around the whole world—by now."

"Yeah, but then you wouldn't have me to help you with your outside shot," Nicholas said, and made a shot so clean it didn't even touch the rim.

"I guess that's true. Growing up in Cottonwood Falls has had its advantages." I shot from outside, and the ball bounced off the backboard. Nicholas laughed and I charged at him. He dodged off the driveway, out of the yellow light, and I chased him across the dark yard until I tackled him and we fell onto the cool evening grass. We lay there in the dark catching our breaths, our arms and legs tangled, and then he was kissing me and I was kissing him back. Not a kiss like the ones he'd given me before, quick and light, but a real, long, deep, swooning kiss. The kind of kiss I'd never experienced before.

"Wow," he whispered when he finally leaned away from me. "What was that?"

"I don't know," I said, grabbing his T-shirt and pulling him back toward me. "But I'd sure like to try another one." And we did. We tried a lot more of them, until Mrs. Blackstone called from the front door and it was time for Nicholas to walk me home.

•   •   •

I checked my e-mail when I got home but had nothing from Kim or Annie. So I sent them a short e-mail, mainly about how I was finally off house arrest and how great things were going with Nicholas. They'd both be home by the end of the month, and I couldn't wait to see them. Right before I hit Send, I added a quick P.S.: *You guys are not going to believe what has been going on since you left. It's way too complicated to get into right now, but it's about my dad, my real, biological dad. I've been in contact with him. Actually, I've been seeing a lot of him. He's right here in town, and I can't wait for you to meet him! See you in a couple of weeks!* I sent the message, then deleted it immediately in case Mom was snooping through my mail. Now that I was sure things were going to work out with Dad, I could tell them. Of course, he might be gone by the time they got home, but I'd met him. He'd found me. He'd be back.

chapter 13

my dad didn't show up at Curry Park for the next couple of days. The weather had gotten hot and sticky, and Vivian wanted to stay home and play under the sprinkler, but I dragged her down to the playground every morning. No matter how much she complained, I couldn't risk missing a chance to see him. I couldn't risk disappointing him by not being there. Even so, when I woke up to rain beating on my window that third morning, I was almost relieved. He'd never expect to see us at the park on a day like this. It was the perfect day to stay inside, but I was restless. I checked my e-mail, but there was nothing new.

Nicholas was scheduled to work at the Nest until late

afternoon, and I tried to think of a strategy to get Vivian down to Riverwood. We could drop in for a latte and scones, and Nicholas and I could figure out what we were going to do that night. And maybe Dad would show up. I was more than a little worried that he'd left again. Had I been too pushy, wanting to see so much of him? He traveled light, he said. He didn't like ties. Maybe I was starting to feel like some kind of leash.

"Let's walk down to Video Barn and get a movie," I said to Vivian. The more I sat around with the rain rattling on the windowpanes, the more I felt like I had to get out of there.

"It's raining," Vivi said.

"You can take your umbrella. You can wear your pink boots."

"I don't want to." Vivian still had on her lavender nightgown, the one with the matching robe that she calls her princess pajamas. She was wearing a tiara and fairy wings and eating a bowl of Froot Loops one color at a time.

"You can get whatever movie you want. *101 Dalmatians*, *The Little Mermaid*. How about *Lady and the Tramp*? Why not get all three!" I said, and realized I sounded like a TV commercial.

"I'll think about it."

"What are we going to do all day if we don't get movies?" I asked.

"Play Barbies."

"I don't want to play Barbies."

"You never want to do anything," Vivian said.

"That's not true." I was about to list all the things I was willing to do with her when I realized she'd done it again. She had me arguing with her on a second-grade level.

After years of experience, I knew arguing would get me nowhere. Only good solid bribes worked on Vivian.

"If we go to Video Barn, I'll play Barbies with you when we get back."

"For how long?" Vivian asked, eating her Froot Loops. She was working on the green ones.

"An hour." I checked to see how much money I had. "And I'll buy you some Junior Mints."

"And Coke."

"Okay, Coke too. If you promise not to tell Mom."

"And popcorn," Vivian said between slurps from her bowl. "I need the kind that goes in the microwave if I'm going to watch movies all day."

"Fine. But that's it." She was definitely getting the better end of the deal—candy, Coke, popcorn, Barbie time, and movies, all for a walk to Riverwood and back.

"Oh, all right." She sighed heavily and went to change her clothes. When she came out of her bedroom, she had on pink jeans and a green T-shirt—and her tiara and fairy wings.

"You can't wear a raincoat over those wings," I said.

"Okay, so I won't wear one."

"Vivi, it's pouring. You'll get soaked."

"Then I won't go." She crossed her arms over her chest, and the wings fluttered.

"Okay, okay, just put on your boots and take your umbrella. A little rain won't kill you, I guess." I slipped on Mom's green gardening clogs so I wouldn't ruin my new basketball shoes, grabbed Tony's big striped golf umbrella, and we headed out the door.

We'd barely left the yard when my dad pulled up in

his blue Mustang. I could hardly refrain from jumping up and down, like I was Vivi's age or something. He hadn't left town after all!

"Hop in!" he yelled. "Rainy Day Taxi at your service to take you wherever you need to go."

"Video Barn," I said as I climbed into the car. Vivian climbed over me and between the bucket seats into the back. Her fairy wings flapped in my face, but I didn't care.

"Be sure to buckle up," Dad said. "Just shove that junk out of your way, short stuff," he said to Vivian. The backseat was full of clothes, camera equipment, a laptop. When he'd said he was living out of his car, I guess he'd meant it. He grinned and looked up at the gray sky. "Pretty dreary day, isn't it? Feel like some ice cream? That's a surefire cheerer-upper."

"Yes, yes, yes!" Vivian shouted.

"If you're not busy," I said, determined not to be clingy.

"Can't do much in this weather! I was just headed over to the Cuckoo's Nest for a cup of coffee. I believe a friend of yours has morning shift?" He raised his eyebrows at me. "How about if I drop you off to grab the videos, and then we head on over for coffee and ice cream for Princess Vivian." Vivian touched her tiara and smiled graciously. It was nice to be in the warm, dry car, the radio tuned to a classic rock station. My dad hummed along with the music, and I wished it were just the two of us heading out of town for Arizona's high desert, where cactus blossoms bloomed like scraps of sunset over dark sand.

He pulled into the parking lot. "Here we are," he said. "Look, I've got to run by the bank. How about if I meet you back here in say five, ten minutes?"

"Okay," I said, getting out of the car.

"Hey, princess." He turned to Vivian, who was still in the backseat. "They give out suckers at my bank. Do they give out suckers at your bank?"

She giggled. "I don't know."

"They put them in a special little drawer and send them to you like magic, but only if there's a special little girl—a little princess—in the car. Would you like to get a sucker?"

"Okay." Vivian bounced up and down on the backseat. Dad laughed.

"I'll take Vivian with me and we'll pick you up in ten minutes," he said. "Then we'll go bug Nicholas and get something to eat."

The blue Mustang had pulled out of the parking lot before it occurred to me how furious Mom would be if she knew I'd let Vivian ride off with Austin Trantor. But what did I care? Mom had been so unfair to my dad. So unfair to me. As long as Vivi didn't say anything to her or Tony about getting a sucker, it would be okay. I'd have to figure out a way to make Vivi understand that we had to keep John, as she still called him, a secret.

Video Barn was packed with bored kids and frazzled moms, and the selection was crummy. I grabbed what I could from the picked-over racks—a couple of old Disneys and Hitchcock's *The Man Who Knew Too Much* in case Nicholas came over that night. The line was long and the cash registers were slow. I watched impatiently through the rain-speckled window for Dad's blue Mustang. I didn't want him to have to wait for me.

It must have taken fifteen minutes to get out of there.

Standing under the Video Barn's dripping awning, holding the movies inside my jacket, I scanned the traffic. No sign of my dad's car. The line at the bank must be as long as the one here, I thought. After five more minutes it occurred to me that he must have parked, so I opened the umbrella and walked through the crowded parking lot, then down the sidewalk to see if he and Vivian were waiting for me on the street. Still no sign of the blue Mustang. What could be taking them so long? By now maybe they were waiting at the Cuckoo's Nest.

I hurried along the puddled sidewalk. It wasn't easy to run in garden clogs, and a blustery wind kept threatening to pull Tony's big umbrella inside out. The rain had gotten heavier, and thunder rumbled in the distance. Coffee and a scone and seeing Nicholas would be just the thing to warm me up.

Nicholas was busing a table near the door. When I came in, clattering the cowbells and dripping water on the floor, he grinned, surprised to see me. From behind the counter Mandy looked right through me, but I didn't care. Ever since the Fourth of July, I knew I had absolutely nothing to worry about from her.

"Hey. What brings you here on this lovely July day?" Nicholas asked.

"You," I said, giving his arm a little squeeze. "And Vivi and my dad." I looked around the room. "Where have you put them?"

He shrugged. "I haven't put them anywhere. I haven't even seen them."

"Shoot. They're probably back at the Video Barn waiting for me. I should have just stayed put." Nicholas looked puzzled. "Don't worry. We'll be back in a few minutes. Save us a table." I hurried out the door, wishing I'd worn some other shoes.

Once again there was no sign of them in the Video Barn parking lot. I went inside and walked down each aisle, Comedy, Drama, Family, but no Vivian and Dad. Could she have talked him into driving her home? If so, I was going to be in big trouble for sure once Vivian told the whole story, which of course she would do after all this confusion. We lost Ginger, she'd say. Who's we? Mom would ask, and then I'd be grounded for a year. I'd have to come up with something really good.

I dug in my pocket for some change and dialed the Cuckoo's Nest from the pay phone just outside the video store.

"Could I speak to Nicholas, please?"

"He's busy." Mandy had answered the phone. I could imagine her in her black tank top, rolling her eyes.

"It's really important, Mandy."

"May I ask who is calling, please?" She knew exactly who was calling.

"It's Ginger. Tell him it's important, okay?"

Dishes and silverware clinked in the background; laughter, people talking. I listened carefully, trying to pick up Vivian's high voice, but I didn't hear it. It took a while for Nicholas to get to the phone.

"What's up?"

"Are they there?" I asked.

"John and Vivi? No, they aren't."

"I can't find them. Unless they went back home." The more I thought about it, the less likely that seemed. "They drove to the bank and were going to pick me up later."

Nicholas didn't say anything.

"Hey, you still there?"

"Where are you now?" he asked.

"Video Barn."

"Look, stay there. I'll be with you in two minutes."

"I'm sure there's some logical explanation," I said, but Nicholas had already hung up. "The computers must be down at the bank." I spoke into the dead receiver. Who was I talking to? I was starting to act a little crazy. And feel a little crazy. I hung up the phone and waited until Nicholas rode up on his bike, soaked to the bone.

"Which bank were they going to?" he asked, not even getting off his bike.

"I don't know. A place where they give out suckers. A place with a little drawer, you know, a drive-through. It's got to be close by."

"Just let me ride around some. You stay here in case they come by." He took off through the rain, spinning an arc of water from his back tire.

I stood outside Video Barn for what seemed like hours. The rain was coming down in sheets. People fought their umbrellas and splashed across the parking lot with newspapers tented over their heads. They'll be back before Nicholas, I told myself. Or maybe they had an accident. A little fender bender in this weather. There had been no sirens, no flashing lights, no sign of a big accident. So it must have been a little one. They were talking with the other driver right now, exchanging insurance information. I kept myself occupied with stories like that until finally Nicholas returned.

"No luck," he said. "Could they be at your house? Did you call there?"

131

"Door's locked. They couldn't get in to answer the phone if I did call."

"How long has it been since you saw them?"

I looked through the rain-streaked window at the clock inside Video Barn. "An hour."

Nicholas looked really worried for the first time. "I think you should call your mom."

"I can't do that. She'll kill me," I said.

"Okay, look, I'll ride over to your house and see if they're there. You go check the Nest again. I'll meet you there as soon as I can."

"Here, take my key. If they're there, let yourself in and call me at the Nest." Once again I fought the rain and wind as I walked along the mostly deserted sidewalk. My feet were soaked and I had goose bumps on my arms and legs. The weather was getting grayer, wetter, and colder—and I was beginning to feel frightened. Nothing was making any sense. I didn't want to go back inside the Nest, so I stood just outside the door under the narrow eave until Nicholas came pedaling up the street. His cheeks were flushed and his hair was plastered to his face. Somehow I had known he wouldn't be phoning.

"I think it's time to call your mom," he said. "Vivian could be in trouble."

"She's with my dad. How could she be in trouble?" I said, trying to convince myself as well as Nicholas. "They're probably doing some other errands. They could be at the Video Barn right now wondering where I am." Nicholas grabbed my hands with his cold fingers and looked at me hard.

"If you don't call her, Ginger, I will," he said, and,

both of us dripping all over the hardwood floors, he led me into a small office at the back of the Cuckoo's Nest. Mandy stared at us as we passed the counter, but I hardly noticed. On an old black rotary phone Nicholas dialed the number of my mom's cell phone. My hands were shaking so badly I couldn't do it myself. He handed me the receiver.

"Hello, Great Homes Realty," Mom answered. "Renee Rosa speaking. How can I help you?"

"Mom?"

"Hi, honey." Mom sounded extra cheery, like she'd just closed a sale. I took a deep breath.

"Mom, there's a problem."

"What kind of problem?" Her voice still sounded cheery, but underneath lay a note of irritation, like maybe she was with a client and didn't appreciate being interrupted.

"Well, the thing is, Vivian's missing."

"Missing? What do you mean, missing?"

"I know where she is, but not exactly."

"Ginger, what are you talking about? Is Vivian lost or not?"

"She's not exactly lost. I just don't know where she is. Specifically."

"Ginger." Mom was starting to sound panicky. "Tell me exactly what is going on!" I didn't know what to say, so I sat holding the phone, hoping that Vivian and Austin would just walk through the door and I could hang up. "Where is your sister?" Mom demanded.

"She's with my dad."

"With Tony?"

chapter 14

"he can't be dead," I said. It was hard to breathe. "I just saw him this morning. He's here. He's with Vivian. They went to the bank."

"Austin died in 1992," Mom said unsteadily. "Of a heroin overdose in Seattle."

"Then who's with Vivian?" I whispered.

"Jesus Christ, Ginger, how should I know? What have you done?" she screamed at me. Then her phone cut out. I sat there for a minute before Nicholas took the receiver out of my hand and hung it up.

"He's dead," I said flatly.

"How could he be dead?" Nicholas knelt down in

front of me. He had both hands on the armrests, kind of closing me into the chair.

"He died ten years ago of a heroin overdose." I started shivering as if I had a fever. "John Arlen isn't Austin Trantor at all. He isn't my father." I looked at Nicholas. "I don't know who he is, but he's got Vivian."

Before I had finished my sentence, Nicholas was dialing 911.

●   ●   ●

By the time Nicholas and I had run through the pouring rain to my house, a patrol car was in the driveway. Tony's truck pulled up just as we got to the front door. I was afraid of what he might say to me, of what he might do, but he ran up and hugged me. He still had on his yellow hard hat, and his face was like concrete, pale and hard.

"At least you're safe," he croaked in my ear, and pulled me into the house, his arm tight around my shoulders. Nicholas followed us into the living room. If Tony hadn't been there, I think Mom might have attacked me. She was frantic. The police officers were having a hard time getting any information from her. All she could give them was a vague physical description of Vivian—dark curly hair, blue eyes. She couldn't even estimate Vivian's height and weight. "She's a sweet little girl, a friendly little girl," she kept saying. "She'd do anything for anybody," she added, and then sobbed hopelessly. Tony took Vivian's school picture off the wall and gave it to one of the officers. An officer asked me what Vivi was wearing—pink jeans, green T-shirt, pink rubber boots.

"And fairy wings," I choked out. The other officer had taken Vivian's picture to his squad car. Two more cars, one unmarked, pulled up in front of the house.

"Tell me about the man with her," the officer said.

"Austin—John. John Arlen," I said. "He's a photographer. He drives this light blue Mustang, an old one."

"Nineteen sixty-eight, black interior," Nicholas added. He sat down beside me.

The officer nodded. "What does he look like?"

Like the picture of my father in the yearbook, I wanted to say. Instead, the words "Blond, tall, blue eyes" came out. I blinked back tears as I described his clothes. "I guess he's about forty."

"Around two hundred pounds or more," Nicholas said. "Long hair."

"Do you know where he's been staying?"

"He said something about staying at a friend's house out in the country," I said, trying to remember the details.

"Or camping at Moose Lake. Or maybe Lake Roosevelt," Nicholas said.

"So he could be anywhere," Mom wailed. Tony put his hand on her shoulder, but she pushed him away. Two more officers in uniform and two detectives came in. One officer asked Tony if there was a computer in the house, while another started taking the phone in the kitchen apart. The detectives introduced themselves as Detectives Zimmerman and Bland. They took over. They asked me a bunch of questions about John Arlen. Where we'd met and when and how many times I'd actually seen him.

"Would you call him a friend?" Detective Zimmerman asked.

"I guess I thought he was. But he told me he was some-one else," I said, barely above a whisper.

"He was using an alias?"

"Austin Trantor." I took a deep breath. "He told me he was my father."

"And you believed him?" Mom shrieked. "How could you be so gullible?"

"Renee," Tony said, "she's just trying—"

"I've talked to you about your father!" Mom screamed at me. "You've seen pictures of him. You should have known better!"

"I know I should have!" I cried. "But you never told me he was *dead*!"

Mom glared at me, then ran upstairs and slammed her bedroom door.

"I don't know how I could be so stupid," I sobbed as Detective Bland took Nicholas out onto the deck.

Detective Zimmerman looked at me. "Did you have a physical relationship with John Arlen?" he asked.

Tony let out a groan, but I didn't get it.

"Physical?" I repeated uncertainly.

"Did you have sexual relations with the suspect?"

I gaped at him. "I thought he was my dad."

"Did you find him attractive?"

"I—no! He's old. He . . ."

"Did he ever make sexual advances toward you?"

"No!" I stared down at my feet. The gardening clogs were spattered with mud. You wouldn't even know they used to be bright lime green. "He held my hand a couple of times. He hugged me once. But it wasn't sexual. He never kissed me, not even on the cheek." I wiped my face

138

with both hands. "I thought he was my father. . . . I thought it was all right."

"What kind of relationship did he and Vivian have?"

"They didn't. She was just there," I said, and then I stopped. "I guess he thought she was pretty. He was always taking her picture. He liked to touch her hair." I could see Vivian in her *Beauty and the Beast* pajamas in his arms, hugging his neck. "He picked her up and stuff sometimes," I said, afraid to look at Tony.

"Do you think she trusted him?"

"Yes. I know she did."

"She thought he was your father too?"

"No—she just thought he was some nice man."

The next hour was a blur of officers and questions and paperwork and phone calls. A police artist came and worked with Nicholas and me to come up with a sketch that looked so much like John Arlen I almost threw up. After that there was nothing to do, just sit and watch the chaos unfold around me. How could I have been so stupid? Tony had aged ten years in an afternoon. His face looked haggard and lost as the detectives spoke to him in quiet voices and took pages of notes. I could hear my mother sobbing upstairs, the sound of the steps creaking as officers went up to talk with her.

And then an officer was saying, "We've instigated an AMBER alert, which will be broadcast immediately. Given the fact we've got such a recent picture of Vivian, and a clear description of the suspect, along with the conspicuous make of his car, there's a very good chance he won't get far."

The officers gathered around Tony for a few more minutes, and then they moved toward the door.

I couldn't get off the couch. Everything seemed unreal. "They said I could go," Nicholas said at last. "I should let my parents know what's happening."

I think I nodded.

His hair had dried in little clumps. "I feel like this is my fault," he said awkwardly.

I stared at him. "How could it be your fault?"

"I should have been more careful."

"You should have talked some sense into me, you mean," I said. "There was nothing you could have said, though. I was a complete fool." Nicholas put his arms around me while I tried to stop crying. "All that stuff he supposedly knew about me, about my mom and Suzanne, I *told* him that stuff. How he met my mom, how he played basketball for Middlebrook—there wasn't a single thing that I didn't *tell* him first."

"He had us all fooled, Ginger," Nicholas said. "I thought he was really cool. I trusted him completely. Hey, they'll find her. I know they will." But he didn't sound very convincing.

I said good-bye and then wiped my eyes. I wasn't going to become hysterical. I needed to focus. If anything happened to Vivian, I'd never forgive myself—and neither would Mom or Tony.

"Please, God, let her be okay," I whispered, saying aloud what I'd been silently praying for ever since the moment I'd realized what I'd done. *Please*.

Tony was making a pot of coffee, not because either of us wanted any but because it gave him something to do. He poured us each a cup and we sat there at the kitchen table, just like John Arlen and I had sat there a few days

140

earlier. How could I have welcomed him into our house? How could I have actually tried to please him with my favorite tablecloth and nice china? I'd even dressed up for him. I'd let him hold my hand. He'd hugged me right here in this very room and held Vivian in her silky little pajamas, held her close.

My throat felt full of dirty water. I made it to the bathroom just in time to throw up. Hot and shaky, I lay down on the cold tile floor.

"Ginger?" Tony called through the door. "You okay? Can you open the door?"

"I'm okay," I answered, but I didn't want to come out. I heard a police officer outside the bathroom door saying something to Tony.

"I'm fine," I called again, a little louder. I don't know how long I lay there. Brushing away the tears, I finally dragged myself up off the floor and rinsed my mouth out with cold water. When I came out, Tony was sitting on the couch.

"It's not your fault," he said quietly.

"It's entirely my fault." I could feel my face crumpling. "I should have known. I should never have let her out of my sight. How could I be such an idiot?"

"You thought you could trust him. Somehow he made you trust him." Tony came and took my elbow and led me to the couch. And then he asked, "Did you really need your father that badly?"

There wasn't a touch of sarcasm or judgment in his voice, only a deep hurt. I pressed my hands against my eyes. I couldn't stand to see him sitting there looking tired and old, his shoulders stooped.

"I don't know what I needed," I said. "But it wasn't this."

Time moved in slow motion. "I should be with Renee now," Tony said, resting his hand on my shoulder. Then he slowly walked upstairs. The coffeemaker hissed on the counter. The whole room looked like it was waiting for something to happen. But nothing did.

chapter 15

suzanne left work and came over as soon as she heard the report on the scanner. By late afternoon several of the neighbors had called, and Tony told them what was going on. Detective Bland said to keep the phone line free in case John Arlen tried to get in touch with us. As the news spread, the phone rang constantly. People were leaving messages asking what they could do. Search parties were being formed. Suzanne was returning calls on her cell phone. I was amazed at how well she handled everything, but that's Suzanne for you. She comes in when she needs to and takes charge. Joyce Davis had organized a bunch of Sunbeams and their moms to post flyers along with a group of our neighbors. Kim's mom and another neighbor came over with casseroles. Mrs. Blackstone sent Nicholas by with a quiche.

"Mom told me not to stay," he apologized. "She's afraid I'll get in the way."

"It's okay," I said. "We're all just sitting here waiting."

And the waiting was almost more than I could bear.

•   •   •

"How's mom?" I forced myself to ask Suzanne. It was eight P.M. She and I were picking at slices of Mrs. Blackstone's quiche on paper plates. Tony was upstairs with Mom. Two police officers were sitting in a car in front of the house, while another was on our computer.

"She's holding up."

"Does she hate me?"

"Oh, Stringbean, of course not."

"But she blames me. She ought to blame me," I said, stabbing my fork into the quiche again and again. "What if we never find her?" I'd seen enough stories on TV about missing kids to know that this was very, very bad.

Suzanne took the fork from me and firmly held both my hands in hers. "Look at me." Her eyes were kind, her voice steady. "Your mother is angry, yes, but she's not angry at you. Mainly she's glad you're safe. This is hard on her, but it's hard on everybody, and she doesn't really see that. She can't see beyond herself right now. She can't see Tony or you—it's just the way she is. Do you understand that?"

I nodded. Still, I wished Mom would ask for me. I

wished she would call me up to her room and let me sit on her bed with her. We could worry about Vivian together.

• • •

That night Officer Stanley stayed at our house. Apparently the police department usually left someone with the victim's family the first night, at least, in case the kidnapper tried to make contact for ransom or some other reason. Suzanne and Officer Stanley and I were watching the eleven o'clock news. Vivian's abduction was the lead story.

"You think he's still around here?" Suzanne asked as the newscaster gave out the number to call if you had any information. Vivian's face smiled from the TV screen.

"There's a good chance," Officer Stanley said. "We've got all major routes covered, the story's all over the media, AMBER alerts have been broadcast throughout the western states."

"It's been twelve hours," Suzanne said, almost to herself. "Twelve hours is an eternity. There's no telling what this monster could have done."

Officer Stanley shook his head. "You can't think that way."

• • •

I didn't think it was possible, but the next day was even worse. Although over a hundred leads had been called in, the police, the sheriff's department, and the FBI had found nothing. Our house was crawling with law enforcement. News vans from all three local stations were parked on our block. Detective Zimmerman stood on the front steps with Mom and Tony as they looked into the cameras and pleaded for Vivian's release.

"We ask that you bring her home safe," Tony said. "Vivian, we miss you." And then he broke down. A couple of reporters tried to talk with him and Mom before they went back inside but had to settle for the neighbors.

By midafternoon, flowers, cards, and teddy bears began piling up in the front yard, and later a group of people with candles gathered on the sidewalk outside our house. The media turned their cameras on the vigil until Suzanne politely thanked them and asked them to please leave. They were driving Mom crazy.

Annie called and left a message. She'd seen the story on the Denver news. Tony gave me his cell phone, but I didn't call her back. What could I tell her? Nothing that would bring Vivi home. Nothing Annie didn't already know from TV. Anything that wasn't on the news I couldn't bear to say.

By nightfall the TV vans had left. Vivian's abduction was now the second story on the six o'clock news, and Officer Stanley was no longer assigned to our house. Apparently John Arlen had no interest in making contact. Suzanne had volunteered to sleep over and stay in touch with law enforcement. A car would be patrolling the area. All she had to do was call and an officer would be right there. Don't hesitate for a minute, Officer Stanley said as he left.

Only Suzanne and I ate Kim's mother's casserole, and neither of us ate very much. Since the news conference,

Mom had refused to leave her bedroom. Tony sat down at the table with us, but after a couple of minutes of staring at Vivian's empty chair, he stood up and took his car keys off the key ring by the door.

"Tony?" Suzanne jumped up and followed him outside. In a minute I heard his truck start up. The engine revved a couple of times, and the truck went past the window. Suzanne came back inside.

"Where's he going?"

"To look for Vivian. She's his little girl. His baby." She turned her back to me and put her hand over her eyes for a minute. Seeing her on the verge of tears scared me. If Suzanne didn't stay strong, how could any of us? I felt like nothing. I wanted the floor to open up and suck me in. It should have been *me* he took. It should be *me* hidden away in some closet or in the trunk of his car.

After dinner I got out sheets for Suzanne. The only ones in the linen closet were Vivian's pink gingham ones. Holding them to my face, I tried to find something of Vivian in them, her salty-sweet little-girl smell, but they held no trace of my sister. I helped Suzanne make up a bed on the couch, then got her one of my nightshirts to sleep in. Tony hadn't come back. Maybe he wouldn't come back.

Maybe he and Vivian would just disappear.

For a long time I lay in bed looking up at the windows darkening until the whole room was black. Vivian hated the dark. Every night she switched on her Winnie-the-Pooh night-light and arranged her stuffed animals in a circle around her. She couldn't sleep without her white bunny and the little yellow chick she'd gotten one Easter.

But the bunny and chick were upstairs on her bed, and she was somewhere lost in the huge darkness. Scared. Crying. All alone.

But she wasn't alone. What was he doing to her? What was he making her do? I couldn't get his piercing blue eyes out of my mind. I couldn't forget his crooked mouth and big hands. And Vivian was so small. He would hurt her. Even if he kept her alive, he couldn't help hurting her.

• • •

I must have fallen asleep, because I thought Vivian was tapping on my windowpane, calling me. Then it was Austin Trantor promising to take me away to live with him in the desert. Then John Arlen laughing at me. And then I was wide awake. For a minute the noise stopped. Then it started again, a tapping, and someone calling me very softly.

"Nicholas?" I got up and opened the window wider.

"Hey, sorry to wake you up. I just needed to see you. I couldn't stay at home."

"I'm glad you're here," I said. "I was having a terrible dream."

"Yeah, me too. Even though I keep thinking I haven't slept at all." His hand was flat against the window screen. I placed mine over it.

"Meet me on the deck," I said, then slipped on a pair of jeans. I felt around for my shoes in the dark but couldn't find them, so I turned on my dresser lamp. Nicholas's picture smiled at me from the corner of my mirror. Nicholas resting his arms on the light blue Mustang, the barn in the background, John Arlen just outside the photograph taking the shot. Angrily I jerked the picture off the mirror and tore it in half. Putting the halves together, I tore it again, hating John Arlen, hating the barn and the car.

And then I stopped. On my dresser top I put the four pieces together again. And I knew.

Gathering up the pieces, I quietly crept up the stairs so as not to wake Suzanne. I took Tony's cell phone from the kitchen table and slipped Mom's car keys off the key ring next to the back door.

"I know where they are," I whispered to Nicholas out on the deck.

"What? You mean Vivian?"

I pieced the four quarters of the picture together with shaking hands as Nicholas shone his flashlight on the image.

"The barn?" he asked. "Yeah, you might be right. He talked about that place enough."

"And photographed it a dozen times at least. And he took you out there to drive his car, right?" I said, a surge of hope running through me.

Nicholas nodded.

"Could you get out there again?"

"Oh yeah, it's easy to find once you know where it is."

"Come on, then. We'll take Mom's van."

"Whoa, whoa!" Nicholas put his hands up. "Don't you think we should call the police?"

"I've got the cell phone. We'll call as soon as we see anything."

"I don't know, Ginger."

"You've got to do this! You've got to drive me out there!"

He followed me to the van, but he wasn't convinced.

"Look, this is just a hunch," I said. "If he's not there, if it's a false alarm, we'll be getting everybody all pumped for nothing. And we'll be pulling officers away from the real search. I told you how many leads they have, right?"

"Yeah, I know. But what if he is there?"

"We'll call 911." I held up the phone. "All we've got to do is check it out."

"This is totally insane," Nicholas muttered as he climbed into the driver's seat. "But it beats doing nothing." He let the emergency brake out, and we coasted onto the street. Tony's truck was parked in the driveway. He must have come in while I was asleep.

Nicholas started the engine but didn't turn on the headlights until we were a block away from the house. The moon was almost full, and the sky was clear. It was amazingly light for three o'clock in the morning. We drove south until we were outside the city limits.

"The minute we see anything we call 911," Nicholas said.

He drove fast. The white center lines ticked away like half seconds under the headlights. I opened my window and closed my eyes against the wind. We are flying to rescue Vivian, I thought. Please let her be there. Let her be okay.

The old barn stood about a mile down a bumpy dirt road. Its silhouette appeared dimly on the horizon. As we got closer, Nicholas cut the headlights. Then he turned off the engine too, and we silently rolled to a stop. There was no sign of the Mustang.

"Doesn't look like anyone's here," Nicholas said. I couldn't tell if he was disappointed or relieved.

"Then we might as well look around," I said. "Maybe he left a clue." The tiara, the fairy wings. Something. As we got out of the van, a second car pulled up behind us. Its lights went off. Nicholas and I ducked behind the van.

"Is it him?" I whispered.

Nicholas grabbed my arm. "I can't tell."

A door opened. A flashlight beam played along the ground.

"Renee?" Suzanne's voice came out of the darkness.

"It's me, Ginger," I called softly. "Turn off the light."

"What the hell are you two doing?" she exclaimed in the darkness. "I thought Renee had taken off in the van, so I followed. But it's you two. You can't even drive yet!"

"Nicholas can," I said, then explained why we were there. Saying it out loud to Suzanne, it sounded pretty ridiculous. I must have been half asleep, still dreaming, when we left the house to believe Vivian would be here.

"Well, as long as we're here, we might as well take a quick look," Suzanne said.

We crept quietly toward the barn, listening. The doors were closed, but through the crack where they met, we could see a faint light. I put my eye to the crack. The light came from a battery-operated lantern set in the corner. Next to it was a brown suede jacket and someone in a sleeping bag.

Then I realized there wasn't just one person in the sleeping bag. There were two.

"It's them," I said, my heart pounding. "He's got her in a sleeping bag with him."

"That bastard," Suzanne said. She grabbed Tony's cell phone and moved away from the door as she called 911. Just then Vivian cried out, a little dream yelp from her sleep.

"Vivi," I whispered.

"Mommy?" she called weakly. John Arlen didn't move. He seemed to be sleeping soundly.

"Ginger, don't," Nicholas whispered. "Wait for the police."

But I couldn't help it. I jerked away from him and wedged myself between the barn doors, which were padlocked near the top but loosely enough for me to squeeze through. Once inside, I sank to my knees and crawled slowly toward her, hoping she knew I was there for her, hoping she wouldn't make any noise. I was ten feet away when John Arlen rolled over in his sleep, his heavy bare arm coming down on top of her as she tried to inch her way out of the sleeping bag. I could hear her whimpering.

"Vivi," I whispered again. She looked up, and I held my finger to my lips. Crawling forward a few more feet, I grabbed her hand and tried to pull her out of the sleeping bag. She wriggled toward the opening. And then John Arlen woke up.

"What's this?" he said to Vivian. "You don't want to go anywhere, babydoll. You're my little girl now." He sat up, his long hair spread over his shoulders. His bare chest was covered with wiry hair and his skin looked loose and paunchy, like an old man's. My stomach caved and I felt like I was going to throw up. When he saw me, he lurched back. "What are you doing here?"

"Dad?" I said, trying to keep the fear out of my voice. "Why didn't you come back for me? Why did you leave me?"

"How'd you get here?" he asked. He was feeling around outside the sleeping bag for something. A gun? I thought, terrified. Or that fancy hunting knife? I forced my eyes to stay on him and not wander to the crack in the door. Suzanne would have gotten a call through to the police by now. If I could just keep him occupied until help came, we'd be all right.

"It's not fair," I whined. "You left me once before, and now you're doing it again."

John Arlen seemed confused. "How did you get here?" he asked again. "Who's with you?"

"Nobody. If Mom and Tony knew I'd found you, they'd be totally pissed off. But I don't care. I don't want to live with them anymore. I want to go to the desert with you."

"How did you know I was here?"

"Don't you remember? How you showed me pictures of this place? How you said it's your favorite place in the whole world?"

Vivian had wriggled out of the sleeping bag now, but she sat close to John Arlen with her knees pulled up to her chest and her head down. She had on only her underwear and the fairy wings, which were crumpled like the wings of an injured butterfly. It was all I could do to keep from throwing my arms around her, scooping her up, and running with her for the door. Why doesn't she move away from him? I wondered. And then I realized that she was tied to him by a short piece of rope.

"Ginger," she said in a small scared voice, "I want to go home now."

It was so hard not to grab hold of her. It was so hard not to scream. But I had to keep focused. "I'm not going home, Vivian. I'm going to live in the desert with my dad. I never want to leave him again." I moved closer to the two of them. If I could just get to Vivi while I kept John Arlen confused, maybe I could untie her somehow. "Can't we just leave her here?" I smiled. "She's not your daughter, like I am. She's not part of us."

A narrow beam of light flashed through the crack in the barn door. "What was that?" John Arlen asked as he jerked around.

"What?"

"That light."

"Just the moon. Can we go now, Dad? Can you take me to the desert?" I kept talking loudly, trying to make as much noise as I could. If he heard someone approaching the barn, who knew what he might do? And I wanted the police officers to hear me and remember we were in there with him. I wanted them to be careful.

"There's someone out there," he said, pulling his hand out from under the sleeping bag. And then I saw the long blade of the shaman knife. The blade flashed in the lantern light. He pulled himself all the way out of the sleeping bag, kicking it off his feet. Stark naked, he lunged toward Vivian. In the dim light he looked like a monster, a gargoyle. I sprang forward. She screamed as the blade sliced through the rope that tied her to him. At the same moment, I threw myself on top of her and felt a searing pain as the knife ripped into my left thigh. The barn door crashed open.

"Stop! Police!" an officer shouted, and pointed his gun

at John Arlen, who was quickly scaling the ladder to the loft. At the same moment, Nicholas ran toward me, and the officer lowered his gun as John Arlen made it to the loft's square opening. Flashlight beams caught his hairy legs and long feet and the dangling piece of rope as he pulled himself up through the opening. The officer fired once, splintering a wooden ceiling beam. I heard a thud outside, then running footsteps, and I knew John Arlen had jumped out of the loft window and was escaping across the field and into the woods.

The officer dashed out of the barn in pursuit, and I looked down at the blood seeping through my torn jeans, and the barn and Vivian's face whirled around in a black fog.

chapter 16

when I came to, I was lying across the backseat of Suzanne's car. Nicholas was holding up my left foot while an officer wrapped something around my leg. A patrol car was parked next to the van.

"It's probably not as deep as it looks," Suzanne was saying to Nicholas. Her voice sounded far away. "Good thing she was wearing heavy jeans. She'll still need a few stitches." I felt the whirly hot darkness roll over me again, but I lay still until things stopped spinning and my eyes cleared. Another police officer on a cell phone paced in the headlights and cast a huge shadow on the barn. The officers stayed with us while other cars went after the blue

Mustang. John Arlen had managed to reach the stand of trees where he'd hidden it and drive away.

"Where's Vivian?" I asked. It was hard to talk.

"Hey, you're awake. Are you okay?" Suzanne asked.

"I'm okay. . . . Vivi?"

"She's right here," Nicholas said. Vivian's head appeared slowly over the front seat. Her eyes were round and unblinking, like the eyes of a frightened rabbit. She was wrapped up in a police blanket, the battered fairy wings gone.

She pointed to my leg, which was bleeding through the bandage now.

"It doesn't hurt much," I lied, and tried to smile. "How are you doing?" She just stared at me with her deep blue eyes, then disappeared into the front seat again. Suzanne helped me sit up.

"That bandage is soaked," she said, dabbing at my leg with her finger.

Nicholas pulled his T-shirt over his head and wrapped it around my leg. Without his shirt, his skin looked marble white in the half light. The image of John Arlen's hairy chest and naked legs flashed through my mind. Not the same, I told myself. It's not the same. But I couldn't look at Nicholas.

"That should help. Keep pressure on the cut," Suzanne told him, "and try to keep it elevated. We're going straight to the ER."

"Take Vivi home first," I said.

She shook her head. "Renee and Tony are meeting us at the hospital. The patrol car will follow us there."

"The officer said we need to get Vivian there as soon as

possible," Nicholas said in a low voice. "They need to examine her."

"Why? Is she hurt?"

His eyes told me we shouldn't talk about it in front of her. "Nobody knows what might have happened," he whispered. "A doctor will be there for her. He'll know what to do."

I burst into tears. When Nicholas tried to put his arms around me, I started screaming at him. He pulled away from me, confused, but Suzanne understood right away what was going on. She jumped out of the car and grabbed a jacket from her trunk for Nicholas to wear.

"I'm sorry," I said. "I don't know what's wrong with me."

"Hey, it's okay," Nicholas said. He sat as far away from me as he could sit while still keeping pressure on my cut. My legs were shaking uncontrollably. "Take deep breaths," he said in a calm voice. "We're almost there."

"I feel like I'm going crazy."

"You'll be fine," Suzanne said. "You're doing great. You are one brave girl, Stringbean. And you're damn lucky you're not dead."

When we pulled up in front of St. Clair's Hospital, Tony's truck was parked right beside the ER entrance. Suzanne hurried Vivian inside, where Mom hugged us and Tony picked Vivian up. Then all three were rushed through some swinging doors while I hobbled into the waiting room, leaning on Suzanne's arm. A man met us with a wheelchair and took me down the hall to another examining room. Nicholas stayed in the waiting room, but Suzanne came with me and held my hand while the doctor put thirteen stitches in my leg. Thirteen, I thought as the woozy blackness rolled over me again. An appropriate number.

Light was dawning when we left the ER. I was so exhausted and spaced out from the pain pills that I hardly noticed the TV cameras. A reporter stuck a microphone in my face and started asking me questions. Suzanne pushed the mike away and hurried me to the car. An officer had taken Nicholas home earlier, so Suzanne and I drove alone through the empty streets.

●   ●   ●

Suzanne situated me on the couch with my leg raised and an ice pack against my thigh. "Want anything? Glass of milk? Coke?" She was holding the refrigerator door open, and in the artificial light she looked like she hadn't slept in days. "I don't know about you," she said, taking out the milk carton and a jelly jar, "but I'm absolutely starved. This rescue work really builds up your appetite."

I smiled at her attempt to lighten things up. "You go ahead. I can't think about food." I closed my eyes. "When do you think they'll be back?"

"I have no idea. You'd think they'd let Vivian get some sleep after all she's been through, poor kid. When they catch that son of a bitch, I hope they bury his ass." I liked hearing her say that. For some reason the anger and passion in her voice made me feel a little better. But not much.

"I can't believe I got her kidnapped," I said.

"Ginger, you've got to stop blaming yourself. *That man* kidnapped her. *That man* assaulted you with a deadly weapon. You are not responsible for the evil that man has done to Vivian, to you, to all of us." She sat down on the couch and stroked my hair. "It's not your fault."

"How could I be so dumb? I must have a brain the size of a walnut." An ostrich brain. And an ostrich eye to go with it. "Why couldn't I see what was going on?"

"You trusted him. He abused your trust." She put her arm around me and rested her chin on the top of my head. "Trusting isn't a bad thing, but it's a scary thing, and we can't always know if it's right. I guess that's what trust is—having faith in something you don't know for sure."

"But I thought I did know for sure. I *should* have known better."

"Try to get some rest." Suzanne tucked Vivian's pink gingham sheet around me. "It's been a long night."

•   •   •

When Mom and Tony came in, Mom took Vivian straight upstairs for a bath and bed. Tony sat at the table with Suzanne and told her what he knew. I was still lying on the couch, unable to move, pretending to be asleep. The pain pills made me feel kind of floaty and peaceful, but I could still hear everything Tony and Suzanne were saying.

"What did he do to her?" Suzanne asked in a low voice.

"There's no physical evidence of anything."

"You mean she wasn't assaulted?" Suzanne blew her nose.

"No, thank God."

"Could she tell the police what happened?"

"She wouldn't say anything."

"Couldn't she remember any of the details?"

"She wouldn't say *anything*. Period," Tony said. "She's not talking at all. Not to me, not to Renee. The doctor said it's not that unusual for a child who's been traumatized to stop talking."

"For how long?" I opened my eyes and saw that Suzanne was crying.

Tony shrugged. "A few days sometimes. Sometimes longer. So far she hasn't been able to tell the police or even Renee and me anything that might help them catch the bastard." He pressed his eyes with the palms of his hands. "All we know is what you and Ginger saw. Plus the police confiscated a camera bag and some rolls of film, but they haven't been processed yet. A police counselor tried to get Vivi to act things out with dolls. But Vivi looked so terrified when the woman asked her to show her what had happened that we brought her home."

I closed my eyes. I was so grateful to have Vivian back. I just hoped we had found her in time.

•   •   •

Not long after that, a detective came to the house to report that John Arlen, who also went by about ten other names, had been apprehended by the Idaho State Patrol just across the state line. He'd ditched the Mustang in a parking lot downtown, but a trucker who had picked him up hitchhiking called in a tip. Detective Alice Martin wanted to talk to all of us, especially Vivian, but Tony said absolutely not. Vivi was finally asleep. She'd had enough questions. So the rest of us—Tony, Suzanne, Mom, and I—gathered in the living room.

Since Tony and Mom had never seen John Arlen, they had little to say. Suzanne gave a clear account of what took place in the barn, but most of Detective Martin's questions were directed at me. Telling her about our later meetings in the park and about the time he came to our house pretending to be my father was the hardest thing I'd ever done. Even harder than talking to Detective Zimmerman right after the kidnapping. Not just because Mom and Suzanne were sitting right there this time, hearing everything I'd been hiding from them, but because I'd had time to think about how I'd turned this man into my father with only three photos and my own stupidity.

Suzanne and Tony kept their eyes on me, nodding reassuringly whenever I looked their way, but Mom gazed steadily out the window, refusing to meet my glance. Other than the hug at the hospital, she hadn't spoken to me—unless screaming counted—or touched me since it had all happened. Detective Martin took her notes without comment, without changing her expression. If she thought I was the lamest witness she'd ever interviewed, she never let on. Instead, she thanked me for being able to remember so many details and for being so candid.

"I can tell you this much about the suspect," she said once she'd finished her interviews. "Along with these recent charges of felony kidnapping and assault, he's wanted in New Mexico for forgery, falsifying documents, and identity theft. He's also under investigation for child pornography. With your help and with evidence we got at the scene, we can probably charge him with that as well."

"Evidence? You mean the photos?" Mom asked. "You've seen them?"

"I have them right here." Detective Martin held out a white envelope. "If you would, Mrs. Rosa, I'd like you to try to identify these for me." Mom handed the envelope to Tony. Slowly he pulled out the photos, and with Mom looking over his shoulder and crying softly, he identified the little girl in the pictures as Vivian.

"There are some other prints at the station, of other children," Detective Martin said. "We'd like you to come down this afternoon if possible, to see if you recognize any of them."

Tony slid the photographs back into the envelope, but he held on to it.

"Mr. Rosa?" Detective Martin said gently.

Tony looked up, dazed. "Yes, I can do that," he said. "Renee might not be up to it." Mom was slouched forward with her face buried in her hands. Suzanne sat beside her rubbing her back.

"I know this is hard for both of you, but your help is extremely important to the case," Detective Martin said. She stood up and turned to me. "What you did this morning was a very brave thing, Ginger."

I nodded, unable to speak.

"You take care of that leg." She shook hands with Tony and told him she'd see him that afternoon.

•   •   •

Tony went down to the police station at two o'clock to look at photos. He recognized one other child—a little boy who lives on the next block, but the photo wasn't porno-graphic. Instead, it was one of those so-called candid por-traits John Arlen claimed to be so interested in taking. There were a few kids in the photos who looked vaguely familiar, Tony told Mom, and he gently suggested that she go down there and have a look. Mom refused. She wasn't leaving Vivian alone again, and she wasn't taking her down to the police station, either. Tony called Detective Martin, who said she'd be over with copies the next morn-ing. By the time she got there, it had been over forty-eight hours since we'd found Vivian in the barn, and she still wasn't talking.

When Detective Martin showed up with the photos, Vivian was scrunched into the corner of the couch clutch-ing her white bunny and her yellow chick. She'd found her old pink baby blanket and had it wrapped tightly around her. Tony carried her upstairs while Mom and I looked through the photographs with Detective Martin. We recognized several other kids in swimsuits, and I knew the pictures had been taken at the Sherwood Apartments swimming pool.

"That's Alex Hoffman," Mom murmured pointing to a photo of a girl in a pink two-piece swimsuit. "And Michaela Ritchie, and Brittany Davis. They're all Sun-beams."

"Sunbeams?" Detective Martin asked.

"It's a scout troop. Mom's the leader," I told her when Mom didn't answer. "These were taken at a pool party they had."

"Location?"

"Sherwood Apartments." They had been taken while I

was right there watching. I remembered how I'd defended him that afternoon, how I'd lied for him, and I felt sick knowing that Mom must be recalling the very same thing. I kept looking at her across the kitchen table, but she refused to see me.

"I'd like to ask Vivian a few questions, Mrs. Rosa," Detective Martin said, sliding the photos back into the envelope.

"I'm sorry, but that simply isn't possible," Mom said.

Detective Martin sighed. "Mrs. Rosa, I realize that you want to protect her, but this is essential to the case."

"Vivi isn't talking," I explained. "She hasn't said a word since we found her."

At that moment Tony and Vivian came back downstairs. "You can try, Officer," Tony said. "If you think it will help in any way . . ."

Mom started to say something, then pressed her lips into a tight thin line.

"Vivian," Tony said, holding her on his lap, "this is Ms. Martin. She's a police officer, and she wants to ask you a few questions." Vivian nodded. Her old pink blanket covered her head like a shawl. Detective Martin sat down on the floor in front of her and smiled. She turned on a small tape recorder and gave the time and date.

"Do you feel like talking, Vivian?" she asked gently.

Vivian stared with her beautiful blue eyes. She looked like a fairy-tale orphan with her head covered that way, a few stray curls peeping out from under the blanket.

"Do you remember going to the barn four days ago?"
Vivian nodded.

"Good girl." Detective Martin smiled and leaned a

little closer to her. "Do you remember what happened before that?"

Vivian screwed her mouth to one side, then nodded again.

"Yes? Can you tell me about it?"

Vivian just stared at her.

"Did you ride around in a blue car for a while?"

A nod.

"Yes. Did you go to anybody's house?"

She shook her head. The interview went on with yes-and-no questions. Detective Martin repeated Vivian's answers into the tape recorder. She was working her way up to the hardest questions, the questions about what had happened in the barn.

"Did the man with you in the car, John Arlen, did he make you take your clothes off?"

Vivian nodded slowly and picked at the raveled edge of her blanket. Her cheeks were blazing red.

"Yes? Did he touch you?"

Another slow nod.

"Yes? Can you show me where?"

Vivian looked at Tony.

"It's okay, honey," he said. "Show Ms. Martin."

She touched her arms and shoulders, her head and hands and feet.

"Did he ever touch you here?" Detective Martin touched her own thighs, chest, lap. Vivian shook her head. "Only here?" Detective Martin asked, touching her arms, shoulders, head, hands as Vivian had done. Vivian nodded.

"Did he take pictures of you?"

Vivian didn't answer but turned and buried her face in

Tony's shoulder. Mom looked at Detective Martin and shook her head. Vivian had had enough.

"Thank you, Vivian," Detective Martin said. "You're a good, brave girl. You want to go to your mommy now?" Murmuring soothing words, Mom carried Vivian upstairs.

"Let me know as soon as she starts talking again," Detective Martin said to Tony.

"It's hard for her," Tony said. "All these questions."

"I know it is. As odd as it seems, given the circumstances, I think she's telling us the truth about any sexual assault. Not all abusers molest their victims in the same way. That's good news. But we still need to learn as much as we can—for her own good, of course, as well as for the good of the case." Detective Martin made her way toward the door. "Unfortunately, I've seen this kind of post-traumatic stress too many times in children. She needs to talk it out. And she will, given the opportunity. I'm not saying you need to rush her. I'm just saying you need to be available to listen when she's ready."

chapter 17

that night vivian's voice floated on the surface of my dream.

In the dream I am in the weathered barn all alone. I'm wearing fairy wings. But the wings are part of me, attached to my shoulder blades. *Am I a fairy or an angel?* I ask Vivian, who is calling my name as I rise toward the loft, light and helpless as a helium balloon. I don't want to go up in the loft because someone is up there, someone who terrifies me. *Ginger,* Vivian calls. *Can I?* She gently touches my wings.

"Ginger? Can I get in with you?" I opened my eyes and saw her face pale in the moonlight that shone through my narrow bedroom windows. "Can I sleep with you?"

"Sure. Sure you can." I slid over and lifted the covers. You're talking! I wanted to shout, but I tried to act normal. "Are you scared?" I asked as she snuggled next to me.

"No, not scared."

"Well, what's the matter, then?"

"I was just wondering."

"Wondering what?"

"I just was wondering why he did that." She was talking about John Arlen. "Why did he turn into a bad man?"

"I don't know, Vivi. It's hard to understand why some people act the way they do."

"Was he mad at me? Did I make him do that?"

"Oh, Vivian, no." I put my arms around her. She felt so warm and little; her hair smelled like raspberries. "You didn't do anything wrong."

"But he was nice and then he wasn't. He gave us ice cream and a picnic at the playground."

"Yes, he was nice at first."

"So what happened?"

"I don't think anybody knows, Vivi. Sometimes people pretend to be somebody they're not. That's what he did. He pretended to be a nice person just to make us like him."

Vivian thought about that for a minute. "But that's not fair."

"No, it isn't," I said. She rolled over and pressed her back into me and slipped her small, hot feet between mine.

"I'll never be that way," she said with a yawn, and went right to sleep.

I lay awake holding her until the windows began to turn gray and I could see my room taking shape in the dawn. Then I took Vivian, still asleep, back to her own room. The last thing I wanted was for Mom, who had been sleeping on Vivian's floor ever since the kidnapping, to wake up and find her missing. My leg was stiff and sore as I slowly climbed the stairs with Vivi in my arms and put her into her own bed. Mom stirred but didn't wake. There would be plenty of time to tell her about Vivian talking. Right now they both needed to sleep. And I did too, but I couldn't.

I felt more tired than I'd ever been before in my life, but I didn't want to go back to bed, so I went out onto the deck and propped my foot up on a chair. The air was damp, and any sunrise that might have shone in the east was covered by a layer of gray clouds. In the woods behind the house an owl was hooting itself to sleep. Sparrows and robins were starting to twitter, and in the big fir tree a flock of crows was tuning up. A *murder* of crows, Nicholas told me once. Not a flock. Once they started, it would be impossible to sleep anyway. I just wanted to sit there alone all day in the damp gray air and think things through.

"Morning." Tony slid open the door and came out onto the deck. "How's the leg?"

"It still hurts. And it's still really gross to look at." The thick gauze bandage was brown and crusty.

"It was a nasty, jagged cut. It's going to take a while to heal. Want me to help you change that bandage?"

"That's okay. I think I'll just sit here awhile."

He pulled up a chair. "Pretty wild couple of days."

"Yeah," I answered. I didn't want to talk; I just wanted to think.

"But it's over."

That wasn't really true, of course. There was still the trial or whatever legal procedure to go through, which nobody seemed to have thought about yet.

"Will I have to testify in court?" I asked.

"If they need you as a witness. I sure hope we can keep Vivian out of it." I nodded. "We'll probably find out soon enough. Detective Martin said Arlen is being arraigned today."

"How's Mom?"

"She's still pretty shook up." Tony squinted into the fir tree, like all of a sudden he found the crows extremely interesting. "She's not really mad at you, Ginger. She just has to settle down. Last night she couldn't stop worrying about your leg. She kept asking if I thought you'd ever be able to play ball again."

"It's not that bad."

"No. I told her that, but she kept talking about it, about you. She's just as worried about how all this has affected you as she is about Vivian."

I didn't believe that for a minute, but I appreciated Tony trying to make me feel better.

"Vivian's talking," I said.

"She is?" Tony exclaimed. "Are you sure?"

"She was last night when she came into my room." I told him how she'd wanted to sleep with me and how she'd been talking about John Arlen. "That was last night, though," I added. "She was still half asleep. Maybe we shouldn't get our hopes up."

"No. Detective Martin's right, though," Tony said. "She'll need to talk it out, but we can't push her. We'll just have to be ready to listen." We sat there until the rain finally started and we had to go inside.

And Vivian did talk about it. That morning, sitting in Mom's lap, she told Detective Martin everything she could remember about the kidnapping. How John Arlen made her undress and run through a wet wheat field and climb on bales of hay while he took her picture again and again. How he took pictures of her in only her fairy wings and told her how to pose and what to do. How he brushed her hair and kissed her face and feet. How he took off his own clothes and made her watch while he touched himself. How he threatened to tell her parents that she was a nasty little girl.

"Did he ever touch you in private places?" Detective Martin asked gently.

"No," Vivian answered. "I know what you mean. Stranger Danger and Bad Touching. We learned it at school. But he never did. He only touched his own self."

"You're sure?"

"I'd tell you," Vivian said. "We're supposed to tell about that."

• • •

Later that afternoon Nicholas came by to see if I felt like going for a walk. He'd called a couple of times before to see how Vivian was doing, to see how we all were doing, but the conversations had been awkward. I felt nervous about seeing him after the way I'd freaked out on the way to the ER. He seemed nervous too as we wandered toward Curry Park, not saying much. We stopped at the pond. A pair of wood ducks were paddling, away from the more common mallards.

"I want to apologize for being such a baby the other night," I finally said.

"What do you mean?" he asked, sincerely clueless.

"You know, screaming at you. Freaking out."

"Jeez, Ginger. Nobody expected you to act *normal*. You'd just been stabbed by a naked pervert. Anybody would be acting crazy."

"I know, but I shouldn't have yelled at you, of all people. It was *him* I couldn't stand to look at."

"Forget it," Nicholas said. He started to reach for my hand but stopped himself.

"It's okay," I said, taking his hand and weaving my fingers through his. "I'm okay now."

"You sure?"

"Yeah," I said, kissing him lightly on the ear. "Yeah, I think I'm okay."

chapter 18

even though vivian was talking as much as ever and the case against John Arlen was so strong that neither of us would have to testify, things were far from all right, especially between Mom and me. I was past trying to figure out whose fault that was. I just wanted us to be able to talk about what had happened, which we hadn't done, not really. It had been days since the police had apprehended Arlen, and she and I hadn't had a single conversation alone. Vivi was with her constantly—or rather, Mom was with Vivian. She was afraid to let her out of her sight and only let her out of the house to visit the therapist. She was still sleeping on the floor in her room, even though the therapist tried to convince her that this was not the way to help Vivian get back to normal. Me she avoided. Whenever we ended up in the same room alone, she found some excuse to escape in a hurry. Tony noticed but didn't say anything. Suzanne noticed too.

"What's up between you and Ginger?" I heard her ask one afternoon.

"What do you mean?" Mom said. "Nothing's up. By the way, did I ever give you that recipe for rhubarb squares?"

Finally Tony convinced Mom to let him take Vivian out.

"She's been cooped up for days," he argued one Saturday morning at breakfast. "She needs to get out."

"I'll go with you," Mom said. "Just let me do something with my hair."

"No." Tony was firm. "She needs to get out by herself, without you, Renee. You can't be watching her every minute of the day. It's not healthy. She has to get beyond this. We all do."

Of course he was right. Vivian did need to get out. But he was also making room for me and Mom to be alone. Making room for us to talk. The two of us stood at the living room window and watched Tony's truck pull out of the driveway. Mom was breathing hard, as if she'd been running. She might as well have been watching Tony and Vivian leaving on a long and dangerous trip the way she lingered at the window after they'd driven out of sight.

I desperately wanted her to say something. Anything. Finally she turned from the window and, without meeting my eyes, pointed to my leg.

"Let me see that cut." I lifted the leg of my shorts and pulled back the bandage. Even though I knew the doctor had done a good job, the black stitches looked pretty un-professional, like the pair of khaki pants Tony had tried to mend once, and the whole area was bruised yellowish brown.

"You'll have a scar there," Mom said, running her fingers lightly along the stitching. It felt strange for her to touch me after so many days of being invisible to her.

"Great," I said. "Something to remind me."

Mom finally looked at me, really looked at me, for the first time in a week. Her eyes had a strange expression, sad and a little afraid.

"I'm sorry," I said. I hadn't meant to be so sarcastic. "I'm sorry. I'll never be able to forget any of this, even without a scar."

Mom turned and went to the window. I thought she was watching for Tony and Vivian; then I realized she was crying.

"Mom?" I took a step toward her. She held up her hand for me to stop.

"I'm going to be all right," she said. "I'm trying to be brave about all this. I'm trying to be sensible and calm like the rest of you. But calm has never been my strong suit."

Calm? Each of us was desperately trying to make it through another day, and she didn't even realize it.

"You've handled this all so well, and I've been a total basket case." She turned back to me, her face wet and red. "Look at you—you're hobbling around with that awful gash in your leg, and I can hardly even bring myself to look at it. You went to the barn, you brought her back, and all I could do was scream at people. You got her talking again. And I'm totally useless. She leaves my sight and I go to pieces."

"Mom, that's not true. You've been great." It didn't sound very convincing, but what could I say?

"I've been awful. An awful mother. Ever since you were little, I've left you on your own too much. And then I left you with Vivian. I gave you too much responsibility. I wasn't here for you when you needed me most. I should have never gone to work last spring. I should have been here."

That was the last thing I expected her to say. She wasn't blaming me; she was blaming herself.

"It's not your fault," I finally managed to say, recalling Suzanne's words. "That man is the only one to blame. That man is the criminal, not us." She raised her hand toward me, and I took it and squeezed hard.

"I should have been more careful," she said. "I've always tried to raise you right, to keep you from making the same stupid mistakes I made. You and Vivian would be open-minded and generous and intelligent. All the things I wasn't. I guess I was so focused on the outcome that I forgot to get to know who you were. I forgot you were anybody except who I wanted you to be."

"It's over now, Mom. Things will be okay."

"No, it's not over. It will never be over."

"You're right," I said, "but we're getting past it."

She wiped her nose with the back of her hand. "God, get me a Kleenex. I'm a mess."

I brought the tissue box from the kitchen and handed her one. She blew her nose hard. Then she smiled.

•   •   •

I wouldn't go so far as to say things got back to normal after that. Vivian still couldn't sleep through the night, and I had weird dreams—naked men crawling through my window with knives between their teeth. To be honest, I still have them. Every now and then, Mom panics and has to see us, touch us, before she can breathe normally again. And Tony is more watchful, more careful.

Nicholas almost lost his job at the Cuckoo's Nest for leaving work the day Vivian disappeared, but after the *Cottonwood Daily Chronicle* reported his part in finding and rescuing her, he became something of a hero around there. I think his publicity has actually been good for business at the Nest, and he's moved up from busboy to barista.

Mom took a leave of absence from work just to get herself together. She's able to go out for more than a couple of hours at a time without completely collapsing now and has gone back to selling houses. Like hotcakes, as Suzanne says.

Tony's been the steadiest of all. He takes Mom's anxiety attacks and Vivian's night wanderings and therapy sessions in stride. I've never really told him about my dreams—why burden him with more bizarre details? And they come less frequently than they did even a month ago. But I have made an effort to let Tony know how much I appreciate him. He's a real father, the only one I'll ever have. Not every man could be a Tony Rosa. Lucky for me, we've got the original.

Kim and Annie both got home in late July. Of course they'd heard all about the abduction on the news. Still, they wanted to know the details, start to finish, from me. I told the whole story—or most of it—once, just to get them off my back. That's it, I said. If you want more, ask

Nicholas. I don't like to talk about it. I was really afraid I'd get back to school and people would look at me funny and talk about how I was the birdbrain who didn't know her own father from a child-porno felon, the one who got her little sister kidnapped and herself knifed, but it didn't happen. The part about me thinking John Arlen was Austin Trantor never made it to the papers. Suzanne said the police are careful not to reveal more than they need to, especially in cases involving minors. Kim and Annie know about it, but even they don't know the whole story.

Even though I know stuff like this happens all the time, all over the place, stuff like this and a lot worse, it's like John Arlen happened to us in an alternate reality, a long time ago. None of it seems possible now.

• • •

One night not too long ago I asked Mom about Austin Trantor again.

"When did he die?" Sadness at knowing I'd never meet him had been replaced with mild curiosity.

"You were about five," she started slowly. "I hadn't heard from Austin in a couple of years. I was engaged to Tony by then, and things were going really well. It was almost like Austin had never been part of my life. Then one night I got a call from his sister, Michelle, a woman I'd never met. She told me Austin had died of a drug overdose in a Seattle motel. I knew he'd been living a wild life even before I lost touch with him, but I couldn't believe he'd gotten himself addicted to heroin. Even then I was so naive." She shook her head.

"Anyway, I said I was sorry to hear it," she went on. "She asked about you, asked if we needed anything, and I told her no. She was very nice. I think she wanted to send you some money, but I didn't feel I could take it without being obligated to her in some way. So I thanked her but said things were fine. And they were." Mom stopped for a minute, then added, "Sometimes I think about that, about how knowing her and the rest of Austin's family might have been to your advantage. They really are quite wealthy. Quite well connected."

I shook my head. "I don't need to know them."

"Well, if you ever change your mind, I'm sure we could get in touch with them."

"Why bother?" I said, looking over at a new photo that hung over our fireplace—me, Vivian, Mom, Tony, Suzanne, and Nicholas at the block party our neighbors threw in Vivian's honor. We were laughing, our arms intertwined. "I've got all the family I need right here."

To learn more about missing children and the AMBER Alert plan, contact the National Center for Missing and Exploited Children at 1-800-THE-LOST or at www.missingkids.com.

about the author

beth cooley grew up in Laurinburg, North Carolina, and earned bachelor's, master's, and doctoral degrees from the University of North Carolina at Chapel Hill. She teaches literature and creative writing at Gonzaga University in Spokane, Washington, where she lives with her husband and their two daughters.